# DIET WITHOUT ANXIETY!
# EXERCISE WITHOUT PAIN!

Are you tired of fad diets and hopeless exercise programs?

JULIUS FAST, bestselling author of BODY LANGUAGE, now reveals in *THE BODY BOOK* how you can cope with the dizzying array of diets and exercises—to choose the total fitness program that's right for you!

Discover your own body self-image, learn about the emotional aspects of eating, explore the world of fad diets, and determine your own diet and exercise profile.

---

## THE BODY BOOK

---

**A maintenance manual
for an improved *you!***

# THE
# BODY BOOK

**Julius Fast**

TOWER BOOKS  NEW YORK CITY

**A TOWER BOOK**

Published by

Tower Publications, Inc.
Two Park Avenue
New York, N.Y. 10016

# Contents

# *Foreword*

It's time Julius Fast was presented an honorary M.D. degree and certified to practice medicine. What are the qualities we most admire in our physician? Thoroughness. Warmth. Patience. Humor. A special empathy that enables our doctor to reassure us as he or she ministers to our pains and misgivings. Julius Fast is one of the few people I know in any field who is such a person.

Here in this book he addresses his considerable intelligence and humanity to diet and exercise, subjects that have been so discussed and written about that they have become a source of confusion as well as obsession. What is one to make of the avalanche of books and magazine articles that tell us to eat instead of drink, drink instead of eat, run and swim or press a fist against our palm to achieve beauty, truth and life everlasting? We need concern ourselves no longer about missing the program that is right for us. Julius Fast has done the homework for all of us. He has read the books, surveyed the periodicals, talked to the appropriate authorities and—wonder of wonders—given us a variety of problems presented by identifiable people who speak for us as well as to us.

He discusses vitamins and macrobiotics, steam baths and saunas, carbohydrates and cholesterol (complete with a handy chart), Dr. Atkins' diet and the Scarsdale Diet. He tells us about Clyde's

paunch and Stacy's success story. With character-
izations that are frequently as humorous as they
are human, Julius Fast has identified a variety of
individual experiences with weight control and
exercise regimes. Clyde's beer belly may be a
source of amusement to his friends, but Julius Fast
listens patiently and sympathetically because he
knows that the distresses of physique are as often
related to the mystery of self-image as they are to
genetic inclinations.

Stacy attributes her loss of forty-three pounds in
five months to the *Fataway* diet Julius Fast introduced her to, but we may suspect from the spirit
radiating through these pages that Julius Fast's
role as the gentle counsellor had as much to do with
her success: "I told her how proud of her I was.
'You look wonderful. As pretty as the day you
were married.'"

Julius Fast brings to his discussion none of the
threats and forebodings of the Savonarolas of the
health business, but he is no Pollyanna either.
Read how vividly he debunks the excesses of a
weight lifter's manual by reminding us that its
author is so peculiarly proportioned he would have
"made Superman slink back into his phone booth
in dismay." At the same time he can recommend to
his friend Susan the gym downtown "which caters
to women who are into weightlifting."

He does not hesitate to inform us when his
health practices are counter to accepted wisdom.
"I prefer steam, but the fact is steam heat can be
dangerous, and the sauna is the safer of the two."

He is a fortunate person indeed who has a friend
or physician as supportive, informed and delight-
fully self-effacing as Julius Fast. It's unfortunate

that he can't get around to all of us, but in the meantime we have the good counsel of this book.

—Avodah K. Offit, M.D.

Dr. Avodah K. Offit is a psychiatrist in private practice, on the staff of Lenox Hill Hospital in New York City (Coordinator of the Sexual Therapy and Consultation Center). She also serves on the staff of the Payne Whitney Psychiatric Clinic of New York Hospital and is a faculty member of the Cornell University Medical College. She is the author of *The Sexual Self*.

# 1

## SELF-IMAGE

### To See Ourselves as Others See Us

There is a philosophical truism: The most difficult task we face is truly to know ourselves. I agree with it, but I think it needs another phrase to round it out. In addition to *knowing ourselves,* we should add *seeing ourselves.* It is extremely difficult for most of us to see ourselves as we truly are, not only in terms of personality, intelligence and talent, but also in purely physical terms. All of us carry around a slightly distorted self-image. I became acutely aware of this one evening recently when I had dinner with two old friends—Anne, who had just divorced her husband, and Selina, who had just married hers.

Selina, tall and very slim, wore clothes well, but, as her new husband said, had "nothing you could grab hold of." During the meal she ate lightly, picking at her food, and afterwards she waved dessert away with a grimace. "I'd love some, but I don't dare."

"Why not?" I asked, surprised.

"I'm dieting. No sweets, no fats, no carbohydrates."

I looked bemused. "Surely you don't want to lose weight?"

"But I do, at least five pounds." Selina patted her bony thighs. "I've got to get it off."

"Why on earth did you go into that?" Anne

asked me later as I walked her home. "Don't you know that Selina is irrational on the subject of weight?"

"No, I didn't know," I answered. "She's so painfully thin. Why would she want to diet?"

"Because she thinks she's too fat."

"Too fat! If she gets any thinner she won't cast a shadow!"

"Well . . ." Anne's voice had a tinge of envy, "she does have a stunning figure."

"Stunning?" I looked at Anne to see if she was serious. A nicely built young woman, Anne had a very shapely and attractive figure—she wasn't fat at all. "If she's your idea of stunning, what do you think about yourself? You don't think you should lose weight too, do you?"

Anne hardly paused to consider it. "Of course. I could easily drop ten pounds."

I tried to explain to her that she was perfect just as she was, that thinner wasn't always better, but I seemed to run into a blank wall. "Oh, men!" was Anne's impatient dismissal. We just didn't understand.

Now I know that Anne wasn't simply putting herself down to invite flattery. She genuinely believed that she was too fat, just like skinny Selina, who believed she should be even skinnier. Is there any woman, I began to wonder, who really sees herself as she is?

To check out some facts about the way we see ourselves, I prepared a questionnaire with three key questions hidden among many innocuous others. The key questions were, *What is your height? What is your weight? Do you think you should lose weight?*

I presented my questionnaire to 100 women in

many different areas. Some of the women were single and some were married; some were house-wives and some working women. I then went over the results with a chart that listed ideal weights for all heights. But long before I was finished—in fact halfway through my questioning—I knew what to expect. Thirty percent of the women were well within the ideal weight range for their height, but only 5 of these 30 percent answered "No" to "Do you think you should lose weight?"

To be fair, I repeated the same test with a hundred men from different geographical areas. A smaller percentage of men were within the normal weight-height ratio, but of these, *all* answered "No" to the idea of losing weight!

"There are a couple of possible answers to why women do not see themselves realistically in terms of weight," said Dr. Fred Klein, a New York Psychiatrist, when I told him of these results. "The most obvious is that what the charts say is the ideal weight is not what the culture says is ideal." At my puzzled look, he explained. "In America today, we are obsessed with thinness. Television, the movies, and above all, fashion show us very thin women as examples of beauty. It's not surprising that eventually we see average as fat and thin as normal."

"You said a couple of possible answers."

"Yes, well . . . another possibility is that these women simply do not have a realistic self-image."

"I'm not sure I understand," I said doubtfully. "Aren't you saying the same thing?"

"No." Dr. Klein shook his head. "I'm saying that there are a lot of people who don't see themselves as they really are. This is not uncommon, and it goes beyond weight. I've had beautiful women patients tell me that they are convinced they are ugly, and strong male patients who are convinced they are weak.''

"And a photo of themselves or seeing themselves in a mirror doesn't work, doesn't straighten them out?''

"What they see in a picture or in the mirror is still filtered through their own eyes and brains. Being objective about yourself is tremendously difficult. Even when you achieve it intellectually, there are emotional factors that contradict what your brain tells you. Most of us reach adulthood with a firmly fixed self-image that doesn't easily change.

"Our self-images are usually created by the way our family and friends see us,'' he went on, "and they become fixed before adolescence. I have a slim young woman as a patient. She was a roly-poly child. All the baby fat, however, melted away at puberty, yet she still sees herself as fat. Like your friend Selina, she never believes that she is thin enough, and of course the culture around her reinforces this conviction. Clothes are modeled by abnormally thin women with bony, shapeless bodies, and she, like all the rest of us, is convinced that skinny is better.''

"But I don't feel men are turned on by these fashion scarecrows,'' I laughed. "At least I'm not.''

"Well, some are, even though it's true that most men are attracted to 'calendar' art; *Playboy* centerfolds; a round, ripe sort of feminine beauty. But all of that is beside the point. You must remember that fashion is designed to appeal to other women, not men!''

I did some serious thinking about Dr. Klein's ideas on a woman's self-image. If many women saw themselves as overweight when they were really normal, what about truly overweight women? How did they see themselves? What sort of self-image did they have?

Diane is more than sixty pounds overweight. She won't confess her true weight, and she is always on a diet of one kind or another. Some of the diets work, but if it's ten pounds off, it's at least eight pounds back on afterwards. "And eventually I even put back those two precious pounds," Diane admitted.

When I asked her about how she saw herself, she shook her head. "Oh, I see myself as overweight, but not fat. I haven't the philosophy of a fat woman. If I wanted to, I could really take the weight off, but somehow I don't care enough to do it. I get along fine the way I am."

Another fat woman, Elaine, told me, "My excess weight has never been a problem to me. Now I'm dieting. I want to take off about thirty pounds, but for health reasons only. As far as appearances go, I'm not at all unhappy about the way I look."

Elaine is married and has three children. She's never found that her weight made her unattractive to men. "Before I was married, I always had boyfriends. Now that I'm married, I feel pretty secure. I have no doubts about my husband."

"He doesn't mind your weight?"

She thought about that for a moment. "He's never nagged me to take any off." She hedged, "I'm a good cook and we both like to eat. He agrees that I should try to lose some weight for my health, but he doesn't want me thin any more than I want to be thin. In fact, I think he finds me sexy. I think it turns him on."

I asked Elaine about her childhood and her family relations, and she told me she wasn't a fat child. "I didn't begin to put on weight until well after adolescence. My father wasn't too happy about it, but he was a real perfectionist. I knew I couldn't please him no matter what, so I shrugged off his disapproval. He made it very plain that being fat made me unattractive, but how could I believe that when the boys I dated all found me attractive?"

Bella, another self-styled "fattie," is a good seventy pounds overweight. Unmarried, Bella is popular, but not on a sexual level. She talks about dieting but never goes on a diet. "I think it's because I hear so much about thin being better, prettier, healthier . . . I know I could never get there, and so I just don't try. To tell you the truth, I find a lot of compensation in eating. When something happens to make me angry, I can always calm down by preparing something nice for myself. You know, I have this conviction that there's nothing food can't cure, including an upset stomach!"

Unlike fat women, fat men find it easier to be accepted by society. Few of the overweight men I questioned saw their weight as a social problem, and none saw it as a sexual problem. Many felt that in terms of health they'd be better off losing some weight, but often there was a peculiar sense of pride involved in this, as if the excess weight they had to take off was a badge of honor.

In an Italian-American community in New York City, one greatly overweight man was pointed out to me with pride by his neighbors. Sal is an important man, a big man. Sal is wealthy as well as fat, a man of substance in all senses of the word, and he carried his weight with pride.

Throughout history, this link between material substance and physical substance has persisted. Stout men have always been well-accepted, and in earlier years, stout women too were considered attractive and desirable. In Calabar, West Africa, body fat was so attractive on women that young girls were kept in "fatting" houses and stuffed with food in order to make them more marriageable. Even today fat is not always ugly. A recent newspaper story about the Tahitian princess Heimataura describes her as "a hefty young princess," an outstanding beauty by the standards of the Polynesian islands, where people of good breeding are expected to eat well, and bulk tends to be associated with high rank.

But most of that is long ago or far away. In America today, stout is out and thin is in—in theory anyway. In actual fact, studies of a cross-section of American women seem to indicate that the great majority, outside of the urban middle and upper class, are overweight.

An interesting fact turned up in my interviews with stout women. Many women who accepted their extra weight and were comfortable with it were working women. One told me that with a job and her independence she began to accept the way she looked. "My fantasies of being thin and a clotheshorse all faded away, and I became very content to be what I was. I had more respect for myself. I was able to accept myself and realize that losing weight was not the answer to my dreams. The funny thing is, once I arrived at that decision, my weight dropped about fifteen pounds, and it's been stable ever since. I'm still overweight by society's standards, but it's no problem for me."

The important fact that I gathered from these as well as from dozens of other interviews, is that how you see yourself is not as important as how you accept yourself.

## Call in the Clowns

We all have the peculiar ability to see ourselves in a number of different ways, and many of us change our self-image in terms of the people we deal with. Take John. At twenty-six, John makes a very favorable impression on his friends and his acquaintances. Talk to him for a while, and you sense a reasonable attitude, a bright intelligence and a pleasant, mature personality. But eavesdrop on John when he is with his parents, and he sounds like a completely different person. His vocal register goes up a few notches, and his voice takes on the suggestion of a whine. His entire posture changes. His shoulders slump, his eyes refuse to make contact and he takes on all the mannerisms of a sullen, unhappy teen-ager.

At home John is a sensible eater, but at his mother's house he seems to become a bottomless pit—all mouth. His mother watches him fondly, and when he hesitates, she urges more food. "Eat some more pie, dear. You've hardly touched your milk." And to his father, she says, "The boy looks half-starved. I just know he's not eating properly. I've told Ellen you're much too thin."

Instead of disagreeing, John reaches for another

helping of pie. Now, which is the real John? Is it the John we see with his parents? And does he wear a mask when he's out in the real world? Or is the real John pleasant and mature, and does he wear the mask when he's with his parents? His wife, who has seen him in both situations, is convinced it is his parents who are at fault.

"Whenever he sees them," she insists, "they do a number on him. He becomes their little boy again, and he acts like a little boy. Leave him with them for a few months and he'd swell up like a balloon. My God, I wish they'd leave him alone and just stay out of our lives!"

But what John's wife fails to realize is that both the mature John and the infantile John are true reflections of her husband. Few, if any of us, are consistent in the personality we project. We present a variety of images to the outside world depending on who makes up that world. A father may be a bastion of strength to his children, but alone with his wife, the same man may become utterly dependent. What he wants from his children is respect, and the strength he shows them gains that. What he wants from his wife, however, is nurturing, and to get that he shows dependence.

In another family, a working wife may be a perfect scatterbrain to her husband, not even knowing how to balance a check book; but the same wife can be a source of comfort to her children, and on the job a competent worker. Each of these "personas" gives her something important, something she needs to feel complete, and for each relationship she wears a different image.

Andrea is a grown woman who is skilled in presenting different images to the world. In her work she is very talented, a fine commercial artist with an amazing sense of color. To her friends at the office she is dependable and serious. But follow Andrea home to her family, and you get a completely different image.

"Andrea is the family clown," her sister admits. "She keeps us all in stitches. She's kind of crazy, but fun, and the outfits she wears around the house —weird!"

I was able to sit down with Andrea one afternoon and have a long, serious talk. My relationship to her included both worlds, the home life where she played the clown, and the business world where she was serious and competent.

Pretty but overweight, Andrea confessed that her "always on" image at home had a purpose. "I know people will like me if I can make them laugh —at least I think they will. I'm not much to look at, and I'm sure I won't get attention by being a quiet mouse. Clowning around the way I do . . . I don't know, it makes me something special. If I can cheer people up, then I really feel like something."

"But you don't clown around at work," I said.

She shrugged. "I don't have to. I'm good at my job and people at the office respect me for that."

Andrea's insight into her own motivations was good, but it didn't go quite far enough. As I came to know her better, I realized that at the base of her problem was her relationship to her parents. A husband-wife team of researchers, Dr. Rhoda Lee Fisher and Dr. Seymour Fisher have studied the backgrounds and personalities of "clowning" children and have found a typical pattern. The mothers tend to be unkind and selfish, and both parents suffer from martyr complexes, generally feeling exploited by their parental responsibility.

They are usually cold and non-nurturing.

In many ways Andrea's parents fit this pattern. Her mother, a very beautiful woman, was uncomfortable in her role as a mother. She rarely showed any open affection for Andrea, and she frequently told her children that she regretted becoming a mother.

Andrea's clowning to gain attention became understandable in light of the personalities of her parents. It was a way of both avoiding and drawing attention to the way she looked. She was very self-conscious of her extra weight and the image she projected. Disguising that image with one of a clown helped mask the real Andrea from her family and friends. At work, the mask could come off because her ability spoke for itself.

It is interesting that the few times Andrea tried to change her image by dieting, she was overcome with panic, especially when the diet seemed to work and a few pounds came off. Then she would inevitably find some excuse to drop it. She felt sick, or weak, or too haggard, or this, or that. The reasons were only important in that they stopped the dieting. Any excuse could serve to get her back to her old eating habits and her excess weight. Her weight was a safety factor as well as a mask.

At home and at work, there were deep, unconscious reasons why Andrea was afraid to show an attractive, sexually appealing and feminine image to the world. The reasons were involved with Andrea's fear of competing with her overdemanding, very attractive mother. Such competition frightened her, and in her inner self, a self hidden so deeply that she did not understand its motivations, she set up all sorts of blocks against such competition.

Any diet Andrea started was doomed to failure before it began. The basic problem was that deep down she did not really want to change her unattractive but safe image. Behind her clowning lay a buried fear of appearing attractive and desirable.

## A Matter of Will

Why is losing weight so easy for some people and impossible for others? A Chicago nutritionist who specializes in weight control told me, "Many overeaters see themselves as victims. They want to see themselves this way because it takes the onus off what they've done to their bodies. A victim has no will power, so these hearty trenchermen suppress their wills—at least in terms of resisting food."

"Then it follows," I said, "that if you expect to lose weight, the first thing you must do is see yourself as someone with will power."

"But will power is a guilt term, and guilt is a nonproductive emotion," my nutritionist friend told me. "Try putting it another way. You must strengthen your sense of self. Someone who starts a diet should also start a list of all the positive things he can think up about himself, mental attributes as well as physical ones. I find it interesting that you used the expression *see yourself*. Seeing yourself realistically is tremendously important in dieting. Self-image—that is really the key. See yourself as only fat, and no matter how much you diet, no matter how much weight you take off, you still have that fat inner vision. You must learn to see yourself as someone with positive attributes, someone capable of doing many things, especially capable of starting a diet and sticking to it. You have to reinforce that inner strength by telling yourself (and believing it), "I can learn to control myself."

"You have to be strong—strong enough to plunge right in. You can't procrastinate and say, I'll start next Monday, or after the next dinner out, or after the holidays, or at the beginning of the month. No, you must start right now! This instant. That's the way the serious dieter does it, the one who'll succeed. The procrastinator is the one most likely to fail."

"But are there only these two types: the serious dieter and the one most likely to fail?"

"Most people who start a diet fall into the most-likely-to-fail category."

"Then they're doomed before they start?"

Smiling, he shook his head. "No, not doomed. Hey, come on, nothing is that certain. There are ways of circumventing fate. But seriously, most people do best when they eliminate the possibility of procrastination or cheating. They succeed when they go on a rigid diet, a diet that tells them eat this, this and this at such and such a time. Eat no more and no less. Don't go off on weekends, or at Mom's house or at Aunt Jo's wedding. This takes away a lot of choice, especially the choice to fail!"

Dr. Joseph Vickery of New York City uses hypnotism for weight loss. He feels that hypnotism is important because it strengthens the unconscious will. People who really want to lose weight but who are blocked from dieting by one thing or another will do well under hypnotism. Those who really don't want to lose—well, for them hypnotism just won't work.

"What do you tell your patients?" I asked him.

"Understand, I don't use a deep hypnotic trance, in fact what I really do is teach the patient self-hypnosis to strengthen his will. I also challenge them as to whether or not they are their own masters." He laughed. "Do they own their own mouths? If they do, they can control what they put in those mouths."

Like the nutritionist, Dr. Vickery insists that it all boils down to a matter of the inner person. "Are you assertive, or are you a marshmallow? If you're assertive with others, then you can be assertive about your own needs. You can own your mouth instead of your mouth owning you. You can also honestly ask yourself, "Do I have to eat this food? Can I forgo the little pleasure that eating it will give me? If I must eat it, why? Why not push it aside?"

"But suppose you're hungry for the food?" I asked.

"Hungry? In this society? That's a cop-out. Sure, some people go hungry, but not your fat dieter. No, it's not hunger that drives him (or her) but a compulsion to eat, a compulsion interpreted as hunger. And what's behind the compulsion can range from self-hatred to anger at the world."

Dr. Vickery was thoughtful for a moment, and I thought of Andrea. I had told him her story. "You seemed to think that most of her inability to lose weight was caused by a fear of looking pretty enough to compete with her mother, but there could be other reasons."

"For instance?"

"Well, I had a similar patient, a fat girl who had always promised herself that once she lost weight, life would be one great song. She would be all the things she wanted to be, popular, healthy, happy—

23

you name it. It would all come true when she reached her ideal weight."

"Did any of it come true?"

"No way! Because she never allowed herself to reach that weight. You see, not losing weight was too good an excuse for not going after all those goodies—and suffering the humiliation of not getting them. She couldn't risk the chance that none of them might come true even if she took the weight off. Better to stay fat and keep your illusions. There would at least be no unfamiliar humiliation. She had already learned to deal with the rejection of being fat. Why face other rejections?"

## The Fat Farm

Turning my attention from adults to children, I went on to interview pediatricians and youth counselors. I discovered that one of the reasons fat children do poorly on diets is that often fat itself can be a way to punish parents. The child's extra weight upsets his parents so much that the child can use his fat as a weapon against them. It gives the child a chance not only to disappoint Mommy and Daddy, but also to punish them.

I discovered that the punishing factor can exist in adults, too, not only to punish others but also to punish themselves. At a recent dinner party I sat next to a young married woman who told me that she had just come back from a fat farm.

"What on earth is that?"

"It's a controlled environment for losing weight. You're given only so much food, made to exercise

24

every day, no liquor or sweets—it's a little like a prison.''

"It sounds like a terrible place.''

"It is, but I liked it.''

"Why?''

"Well . . . '' She chewed her lip a moment. "It made me feel less guilty. I felt that I deserved to be punished for getting as fat as I was, and the punishment satisfied me.'' She giggled suddenly. "It's funny. Usually I feel guilty as hell if I break a diet, but one night three of us sneaked off and pigged out on ice cream in the nearby town. You know, I didn't feel a bit of guilt at the binge!''

The prisonlike atmosphere of the fat farm helped assuage her guilt feelings, I was sure. She was being punished, so why not commit a "crime''?

The punishment of fat can also be directed at someone else. Like the child who punishes Mommy and Daddy, the adult can become fat and stay fat to punish a wife or husband, or being fat can go beyond this and become a way of getting back at the world. "Everyone wants me to be thin, to lose weight. Well, to hell with everyone!''

Here the excess weight stays on as an act of rage or hostility at everyone. And yet, with the rage there is often a need for gratification. I'll take care of me. I'll eat for comfort; who cares what anyone thinks?

Still another cause of overeating, close to self-gratification, is the nurturing aspect of food. Stuff your own belly and you are being good to yourself. You are nurturing yourself. You become your own "Jewish mother,'' telling yourself, "eat, eat and you'll feel better.'' The very act of eating can be soothing and comforting, a reason why so many overeaters turn to food when they are upset.

Often, behind overeating there is an element of despair. People who have given up on gaining approval from others may overeat just to convince themselves that they don't want the approval anyway. If they don't want it, their logic tells them, then obviously they don't need it. The dinner plate becomes the closest friend they have.

## Dieting to Death

Steven Levenkron, who works at New York's Montefiore Hospital Department of Pediatrics in the Division of Adolescent Medicine, deals with problems of overeating and with anorexic girls. He points out that while overeating can be a sign of anger, refusing to eat can also be an aggressive act or a way of relieving anxiety. "It is self-destructive," he told me when we discussed the problem, "even though people who refuse to eat or diet obsessively aren't trying to hurt themselves, not deliberately. As a matter of fact, they start their dieting as a self-protective measure."

"What happens then?" I asked.

"Something goes wrong and what was once self-protective—a way of losing excess fat—becomes self-destructive. This is what happens to anorexics, and any book about dieting must include a warning against this frightening syndrome."

Anorexia Nervosa is a very terrible disease that strikes young women and occasionally young men. It is a disease in which people literally starve themselves to the point of emaciation. The anorexic may start as an overweight young woman, but along the line something happens to her perception of herself, her self-image, and she continues to see herself as plump or fat even when she becomes as wasted as a survivor of one of Hitler's death camps. She desperately tries to diet away breasts and thighs that are no longer there. It is a pitiful illness and very dangerous for the anorexic. Without help, and often even with help, she can diet herself to death.

Levenkron, I know, has had an extraordinary cure rate in treating this disease. "Anorexics," he explained, "usually start by dieting to protect themselves from becoming too fat. At no point in the progression of the illness do they see the reality of their body image."

"I find that hard to understand," I protested after seeing some disturbing pictures of anorexic girls. "Surely a good look in the mirror will show them their own emaciation."

"You're talking reality. As you know, not everyone sees the reality of his or her own body. Even mentally healthy people have difficulty seeing themselves. Haven't you known beautiful women who thought they were plain, or ugly men who considered themselves handsome?"

"But that's not quite the same."

"On a small scale it is. Anorexics are prevented from seeing their image realistically because they take an idea and cling to it at the expense of proportionate reality."

"I'm not sure I understand that, but it seems to me," I said slowly, "that society must play a big part in this whole problem. Isn't there a constant pressure on women to be thin? All the advertisements, television, the movies and fashion keep insisting fat people are laughable; thin people are admired."

"Oh yes, the social pressure is enormous, but all young women are exposed to that pressure. Only the anorexic personality succumbs."

*The anorexic personality.* How can you tell if you, or your teen-age child is vulnerable? How do you describe the anorexic personality?

Based on what Levenkron said, I believe that a profile for a teen-ager in danger of becoming anorexic could be constructed. It is usually a girl, although some 5 percent of anorexics are boys. The potential anorexic is a bright child with an obsessive edge. She tends to intellectualize, to over-think, and she is very manipulative. In one sense, her weight loss is a way of controlling her parents, and if hospitalized, her doctors and nurses. She clings to ideas and procedures rather than to people. She is rigid, afraid of change, has difficulty in making decisions and is overconcerned about the opinions of others.

"Dieting," Steve Levenkron told me grimly, "is serious medicine, especially for someone like that, and in a sense, it is serious for all adolescents. I wouldn't let any teen-age child of mine diet without medical supervision."

What is implied in Levenkron's warning is the extreme danger of changing your physical appearance during adolescence. Adolescents define themselves in terms of how they look, how they dress, how fat or thin they are. Their developing bodies are at once a source of excitement and a source of fear. A young girl may desperately long for her breasts to develop, even while she is ashamed of their appearance. A young man is eager for his genitals to mature, and yet there is a sense of shyness mixed with a fear of inadequacy as they

28

develop. The maturing body is nothing to tamper with, and a diet at this point, particularly a fad diet that deprives the body of necessary nutrients, can be disastrous. I have to agree with Levenkron that any teen-age child on a diet should be supervised by a doctor or a good nutritionist.

And still, at this time of life, teen-agers, especially girls, are deluged with a media blitz designed to change their image in terms of the unreal standards set by fashion. The severest standard is weight loss. You cannot have any sort of social life, according to all the ads, unless you are thin, and models who are as gaunt as skeletons are draped with the current fashions to prove it. Every woman's magazine has at least one article on hair style or makeup, all with before-and-after pictures to explain how important it is to change your image.

It is difficult, if not impossible, for the average teenager to resist this media blitz completely. Everyone gives in to it to some degree, but those who are able to resist it best have firm, supportive parents—a father and mother who allow some leeway and may tease a bit about hair, clothes and figure, but who are decisive when it comes to any serious dieting or any inappropriate clothing. They may be a bit old-fashioned, but they are exactly the kind of parents who can buttress a teenager against the flood of social pressure to dress one way, make up another.

The uncaring parents who shrug off parenting and let their child "do his own thing" or "make his own decisions" are the ones who relinquish their parental role to society. The culture then becomes the final arbiter in what is right and wrong for the teenager . . . and trouble begins.

Fortunately, the dieter who ends in anorexia is a rare problem, and of course not every victim of anorexia dies. On the other hand, not every anorexic grows out of it. Some do, surviving and getting over it completely. Others live in continual danger of falling back into the anorexic pattern. Anorexia is not a cut-and-dried condition. There is one form in which the victim will go on eating binges followed by induced vomiting. The eating binges usually start after a severe diet. After the binge comes guilt, and after the guilt a compulsion to lose weight by fasting, dieting, constant vomiting or even laxative pills.

Steven Levenkron, as well as many psychologists, warned that before starting a diet, you must know something about yourself. You have to understand your inner motivations. This is not only imperative for potential anorexics, but also for people who are simply overweight. It is very destructive to the self-image of a fat person to start a diet and fail. It will happen again and again to certain people, and each time it happens it confirms their own conviction that they are losers.

In searching out the factors that make for a successful diet, I began to realize that there is a set of questions you can ask yourself, a sort of dieter's test, that will help you decide whether or not you are a good candidate for a weight-loss diet. We will go into this in the next chapter.

# 2

## CULTURE, EMOTION AND EATING

### How Many Meals a Day?

Why do we overeat? Why is it that when the belly is filled, the mouth often keeps on working, and the hand keeps lifting the fork to shovel food in? Hasn't nature built in some control to tell us when we're full just as she tells us when we're hungry? And if there is one, why does it work so poorly in so many of us?

There is a great deal of evidence that the sugar balance of the body, the level of sugar in our blood, is the machine that controls our appetites. When the sugar content gets below a certain point, our hunger clock goes off and we start to look for food. When it reaches a higher level we feel full and we stop eating.

At least some anthropologists surmise that that is how it was in those vague, primitive days when most of man's waking life was concerned with gathering food or hunting. As civilization took over and people gained control over their sources of food, it was more convenient to regulate meals. Mankind gave up eating all the time, eating catch-as-catch-can, and life began to fall into logical divisions. Breakfast, lunch and dinner—and in some hungrier cultures, brunch, tea and supper were added.

Today's world generally opts for the three-a-day pattern—when the food is available. However, we are not all built the same way, and many of us have hunger clocks that won't adjust to the three-square-a-day routine. We're hungry too soon or hungry too late, or hungry too often or food gets tied up with socializing, and we fall into that tender trap, the off-meal snack.

"I could keep my weight down very easily," Nell confided to me, "if it weren't for those goddamned coffee klatches!"

"Must you have them?" I asked.

Nell rolled her eyes dramatically. "Oh Lord! You don't know what it's like raising a family in the suburbs, seeing only kids all day long." She bent quickly and hugged Bobby, her eight-year-old. "Not that I don't love you madly, baby, but if I didn't have some adult company I'd go bonkers. I love getting together with the girls in the neighborhood. But when we get together it's just expected that whoever's house it's at will lay out the cakes and Danish and coffee, or little sandwiches. It even gets to be competitive. Who can turn out the best snacks. Maybe it's because our days are so empty."

Her husband, Bob, shook his head. "Hey, you're not the only one who's a prisoner of food. What about our coffee breaks when that cart comes around with the packaged cakes and candy bars—ten in the morning, and then again at three-thirty. I talked to our office manager about it, but he put me down. Claims we get low blood sugar around then and need the refreshment."

"Can't you work through the coffee breaks?" I asked.

"Not bloody likely. They're social breaks too.

I'd be labeled offbeat, antisocial, and anyway, they serve a purpose of sorts. Besides nourishing our bodies, they nourish our minds." At my blank look, he explained, "We trade ideas during the breaks."

Bobby, who had been listening attentively, put in his two cents worth. "You guys think you're the only ones who have to lose weight, but I have to too. Our swimming coach told me I'm too fat in the butt!"

"He didn't!" Nell was shocked. "Wait till I have a word with him."

"Hey, Mom, no way! Besides, he's right. Every time I come home from school you stuff me full of cookies and milk. Daddy has his coffee break, and you make me take a milk break."

"Don't you like it?"

"I love it." He frowned. "But do I need it, Mom? Do I?"

Thoughtfully, Bob said, "You probably don't, son. Any more than Mom and I need our eleven o'clock snack in front of the TV while we watch the news. Nell, you ought to talk to the pediatrician about that. Are we really stuffing the kid?"

It occurred to me, after Bob's mention of TV, that television itself fosters this snacking concept. You can't have a really good time in TV-Land unless there's a chest of cold beer, or Coke, or Pepsi, or Dr. Pepper or some other drink. All those fun-loving young men and women who are constantly passing drinks around as they exude charm and joy. In TV-Land mothers are always preparing after-school snacks with "wholesome" cupcakes or cheese or peanut butter or this or that. I could hardly blame Nell and Bob, considering the indoctrination they were getting.

To many people the mouth, instead of the body blood sugar, has become the mechanism that sets off hunger. It isn't a case of the body needing the nourishment, but of the mouth needing the oral gratification of chewing, tasting and swallowing. Once this begins to happen, some people lose their ability to cut off hunger when the body has enough food. Hunger becomes a symptom of other needs instead of being a need in itself. Satisfying hunger is the same as satisfying a lack of love, unhappiness, boredom. Eating shall make you free, the mouth tells the body, and the body compliantly shoves food into the mouth.

## The Trouble With Taste

Another problem that has developed along with our three-meal culture is the psychological aspect of eating and overeating. As society became more complex, the meaning of eating went through subtle changes. Instead of food being served for survival, food was served for status, or for pleasure, or even to comfort someone in pain. In some people, eating was linked to guilt while in others it was tied to love and affection. The giving of food came to be equated with nurturing. Emotions have had an influence on the eating patterns of many people, and obesity has become one of the sad results of all this stuffing, of all the eating after the hunger clock warns the body that it is satisfied.

In still other people, eating has turned into an answer to anger, to rage. In a recent interview, Albert Innaurato, the man who wrote *The Trans-*

*formation of Benno Blimpie* (a play about a grossly obese young man), talked of his own problem of overeating. "I'm a crazy eater," he declared. "I mean I eat because I get crazy. It has a lot to do with hostility and rage. I have a terrible temper, and if I eat something when I get angry it helps me." Defensively, he added, "It's better than running out and killing someone."

Marcia Millman, author of *Such a Pretty Face*, subtitled *Being Fat in America,* is another person who has a personal weight problem. She agrees with Innaurato's concept of anger as a driving force in overeating. "Some women," she states, "have naturally plump bodies and can't slim down, or have just developed bad eating habits." She feels that these women become upset over their weight because society has such restrictive standards of what's acceptable.

"They turn to food out of frustration and anger because they feel unfairly treated," she said, but noted that the extra weight they put on only intensifies their frustration.

Another problem of overeating comes from the fact that we do not all respond to food in the same way. Take a young couple I know, Naomi and Perry. They've just been married and seem to get along well on every marital level except one—eating. Naomi, round and delightful in her curves, seems always to hover on the edge of plumpness. Gaining weight is a constant terror. Perry, lean and muscular, has absolutely no weight problem. But then, their eating habits are different.

"I don't understand Perry," Naomi confided to me. "I like to eat. I like the taste of food. It gives me a great deal of joy. Before we were married, one of my biggest treats was eating out at different restaurants. Discovering a new taste in food was always such an adventure, so much fun. Now, with Perry, all the joy is gone out of it.''

Perry presented his side of the problem. ''I don't understand Naomi. I don't understand her excitement in a Chinese restaurant. I eat because I'm hungry, just as I breathe because I need the oxygen. I don't get excited about a new kind of air, so why get all hepped up about a new kind of food? It all tastes pretty much the same.''

The last statement of his alerted me to a possible problem. I dragged Perry and Naomi off to the laboratory of a chemist friend of mine. Sam was doing research in the genetics of tasting. At my suggestion, he administered the PTC test to both Perry and Naomi. Now PTC is short for phenyl-thiocarbamide, a bitter substance to some people. Naomi and I found that it tasted bitter. Naomi, in fact, could hardly bear it. When Perry tasted it— or rather failed to taste it—he shrugged. ''No taste at all.''

Sam nodded. ''That could probably be at the root of your different eating patterns,'' he explained to the two of them. ''You see, PTC is bitter to some people and tasteless to others. The inability to taste it is genetic, a simple Mendelian recessive trait. If you have two recessive genes for PTC-tasting, you are relatively insensitive to the substance. One or more genes allows you to taste it.''

''How many people can taste PTC?'' I asked.

Sam laughed at that. ''You three carry out the national average. Two out of every three people can taste it. Some people are super-tasters. They find PTC extremely bitter.''

''I did,'' Naomi screwed up her face. ''I was just

shocked that Perry couldn't taste it at all."

"It was mildly bitter to me," I said.

"Well, there you have it. Nature provided some of us with this sensitive tasting sense as a survival factor. Most poisons are bitter and being able to taste bitter things helps us avoid them. In simpler times it was an evolutionary plus.

"You know, it's a funny thing," he went on. "People with this genetic ability to taste PTC may also find coffee bitter and need milk and sugar to take the bitterness away. The caffeine in coffee is a bitter substance, and there is just enough of it in freshly brewed coffee to trouble a sensitive PTC taster."

"But on an overall basis," I asked, "could Naomi's keen ability to taste PTC account for her love of food, and could Perry's inability account for his indifference?"

"It's very possible," Sam said. "Very possible. You know, we chemists involved in the science of tasting believe there are only four basic tastes: sweet, sour, salty and bitter—and all the combinations thereof."

"But surely there are others," Naomi interrupted. "What about . . . well, chocolate or vanilla?"

Sam smiled. "Good thinking. They're different, but properly speaking, they aren't tastes. They belong to a different category as you'd realize if you tried to taste them when you had a cold in the nose. They are smells. We smell them instead of taste them. And there's another reason why some foods taste different to different people. Certain foods affect our taste buds. The berries of a tropical plant with a mouthful of a name, Syncepalum dulcificum, aren't much themselves, tastewise, but they can affect our taste buds and make some sour foods taste sweet. Artichokes, after they're eaten, will make some people find other food sweeter. And other substances beside food affect our taste. Take toothpaste. If it has detergent in it, it can destroy the phospholipids on our taste buds and make our morning orange juice taste sour and bitter.''

I was surprised. ''That's often happened to me in the morning. I thought it was the brand of juice. Maybe now I should brush my teeth after breakfast.''

''Or else make sure your toothpaste hasn't sodium laurel sulfate in it. It's a funny thing, but some people have saliva that has a similar effect on the taste buds. It can change the taste of salty substances. What I'm saying, really, is that it's very possible that both Naomi and Perry taste foods differently. Perry may find food dull and ordinary, while Naomi finds the same food exciting and delicious.''

We had to be satisfied with that. There's no arguing with taste. Naomi and Perry solved their problem when she began saving her working lunches for all her ''exciting'' eating, and they prepared ordinary healthy but bland food at home. ''Perry is satisfied, and I get my exotic tastes during the day.''


## One Man's Meat . . .

Whether it's genetic or not, there really is no accounting for taste. It may be due to different receptors in our mouths, but it may also be due to different receptors in our brains. ''Have you ever wondered," a psychiatrist friend asked me, "why, as a nation, we don't eat foxes, dogs, cats or horses?"

I started to say because their flesh tastes bad or too gamey, but then I caught myself. I remembered a story my son told about his six month's stay in Costa Rica working as a geologist for an archeological dig. "We were subsisting very low on the hog," Tim told me, "so low that we had to live in native quarters, eat in native restaurants and even drink in native bars. One evening a group of us went to the local cantina and started belting down tequila with lime and salt. We were having a great time—I'd come to love tequila—when I noticed that a bowl of munchies had been put out on the bar for us to nibble on between drinks. I nibbled away happily while we all argued about the damage a local earthquake had done to the digs that morning. When the bowl of munchies was gone, I asked the bartender for another. 'What are they? They taste delicious.'

"He put a fresh filled bowl next to me and grinned, pleased that I liked them so much. He explained in Spanish what it was and I realized I had been gorging myself on bits of deep fried cat meat!"

"The answer," I told my psychiatrist friend, "is undoubtedly cultural."

He nodded. "Exactly. You know, there was a time when the Russians ate fox and the Chinese ate dog and we have eaten horsemeat in America—it's indeed a cultural thing, but so is the structure of our meals."

I looked puzzled, and he explained. "In our culture meals have a beginning, a middle and an end. An appetizer, perhaps a soup, a salad, a main dish, then dessert and coffee When we see the coffee come, we know that the ___ is over. And we are psychologically filled up. Do you know why Americans feel hungry a short time after eating Chinese food?"

"Because of the way it's cooked? I mean with small portions of meat," I ventured.

"Not at all. I believe it's because we haven't adapted Chinese food to our own Western meal structure. We miss that big main course, the way our meals build and decline. True Chinese food consists of a number of equal portions of food." He hesitated, "Though most Chinese restaurants serve appetizers and dessert to trade in on our western patterns."

"But how would that make us hungry a few hours afterwards?"

"The structure of the meal doesn't send us a signal of completion. It's the same with Indian meals, which depend on a spatial arrangement—certain foods arranged on the right, center and left of the dish. In America we arrange our food on a temporal basis, beginning, middle and end. So it's not only what the meal contains that satisfies hunger, but also how the meal is structured."

His words came back to me recently when I watched the TV performance of *Shōgun,* James Clavell's dramatized novel about Japan in the 1500s. The series was accurate in its comparison of sixteenth-century European culture with that of Japan, particularly in terms of food. One of the telling points made was that Europeans hung game until it was fetid, putrid and tender. In the TV film, the Japanese can't abide the terrible odor of hung gamebird, and a servant removes a hanging bird even though the act costs him his life.

Nowadays we rarely, if ever, hang game birds or beef. The rank, gamey odor once so prized is distasteful to our twentieth-century palate. Perhaps, as cultures become more intricate, tastes become blander. Sixteenth-century Japanese culture seemed in many ways advanced beyond the European. Perhaps not technically, but certainly in terms of intricate customs and mores.

Professor Mary Douglass, director of research and culture at the Russell Sage Foundation, believes this change to a bland taste is a sign of advancing civilization. "Creamy, fresh Gorgonzola cheese is now preferred to Gorgonzola crawling with maggoty life," she states, pointing out that the riper kind was once most popular. "Once we realize that ideas of edibleness are rooted in culture, we can speculate about food revolutions of the future." She suggests that we may someday reject the idea of breeding and killing animals for food. "Or we might change our attitude towards the edibleness of vermin and bugs." This, she concludes, would enable the human race to feed on its own parasites and pests!

It's worth thinking about, because even today there are cultures in the South American jungles who find maggots and bugs a fine source of protein. We consider them primitive, but one race's primitivism is another's sophistication, especially in terms of food!

## The Emotional Test

In this chapter, we've seen how our emotions—anger, love, unhappiness—can all influence our patterns of eating and our ability to take off weight —or our inability.

Dr. Richard Kozlenko, a California physician and biochemist, is a firm believer that very often (too often in fact) the emotions overpower the subtle body clues, such as blood sugar, that tell us we have had enough or too much to eat. In attempting to single out the people who are most readily affected by emotions in their eating patterns instead of by direct hunger, Dr. Kozlenko has prepared an elaborate questionnaire and test. I have reworked a brief section of this test and added some other questions suggested by various psychologists involved in weight loss and dieting.

By testing yourself you can decide whether emotional interference plays havoc with your eating patterns. There are five degrees of involvement. (0) *Never*. This is fairly obvious. You just never do these things! (1) *Seldom* means roughly from four times a year to once a month. (2) *Occasionally* would be two to three times a month. (3) *Often* is from one to three times a week, and (4) *Very Frequent* is every day, or every other day.

To take the test, read each box on the left carefully, and then consider your own attitudes and habits as honestly as you can. This test is only effective if you can be honest and objective about yourself. Then in whichever box on the right fits you, place the number that appears at the top of the column. For example, if you are always the first one finished at every meal, you would put a 4 in the appropriate box.

| | 0 | 1 | 2 | 3 | 4 |
|---|---|---|---|---|---|
| **Are you the first one finished at every meal?** | | | | | 4 |

Starting with the first question, answer each and score yourself at the right.

| The foolish things you do | How often you do them | | | | |
|---|---|---|---|---|---|
| | 0 | 1 | 2 | 3 | 4 |
| **When you're bored or depressed, do you begin to eat?** | | | | | |
| **Do you ever get that oh-to-hell-with-it-all feeling and head for the bakery or ice cream parlor?** | | | | | |
| **Did Mommy or Daddy give you cookies or candies as rewards?** | | | | | |
| **When you're thinking of something else do you find that you've opened the refrigerator and are staring at the contents?** | | | | | |
| **All it takes for you to eat something is to have your mother, father, husband or wife tell you it's bad for you.** | | | | | |

| The foolish things you do. | How often you do them. | | | | |
|---|---|---|---|---|---|
| | 0 | 1 | 2 | 3 | 4 |
| Do you eat goodies when you know nobody can see you, in the car or when you're out for a walk? | | | | | |
| Do you detest the mirror in your house and wish you looked different? | | | | | |
| Are you the first one finished at every meal? | | | | | |
| Do you have those secret little orgies where you pig out on some luscious food? | | | | | |
| Do you consider sweets the greatest invention since the wheel? | | | | | |

## SCORING

Score the indicated points 1, 2, 3, 4 or 0 in the boxes after each foolish thing. Then add up all the points and multiply by three. If your total score is 60 or less, then you understand your physical needs and you have a good relationship with yourself. The odds are you don't need to diet, or if you do, it's going to be pretty easy to knock off those extra pounds.

If your score is anywhere from 61 to 80, you are in the average range. There's nothing really wrong with you that isn't wrong with any normal, healthy person.

If you hit between 80 and 95, watch out! There is

a little too much emotion guiding your eating habits.

And if you score above 95 you're in trouble. Your emotions are controlling the way you eat. If you're not too fat, you will be. Dieting is going to be something of a problem.

Now once you realize the exact role emotions play in your eating habits, it's time to discuss whether or not you're a good candidate for a weight-loss diet. Is dieting going to be easy or hard? You should know this before you start because it may affect the diet you choose. No matter how difficult weight loss may be, it's almost never impossible. The old excuse, "My glands won't let me take off fat," is just that—an old excuse. It may have done for your grandparents back in the days when full, over-ripe women and stout men were admired, but it won't do for you. In the first place, glandular problems that prevent weight loss are exceedingly rare. If by some remote chance that *is* your problem, a good endocrinologist can help you out. In the second place, it's much more likely that any glandular imbalance you might suffer is due to the excess weight you're lugging around, and dieting it off may very well straighten out those pesky glands.

The real problem behind extra weight is almost always emotional. Now if you are overweight, ask yourself some soul-searching questions. Do you feel a sense of desperation about your extra weight? If you do, score one for emotion. A second question: What do you think of yourself as a person and how do you see yourself? Do you feel good about yourself? Honestly, now, what do you *really* think? No one but you will hear the answer. On a scale of one to ten, if you rate yourself below eight, then self-image is one of your problems. The chances are also good that your self-image is false, that you are a much better person than you think you are.

Another searching question: Do you really feel loved and cared for by your husband, wife, children or parents? Again, if you answer "No," this can be a very important reason why losing weight is so difficult for you.

While we're on the subject of the interior *you*, and your close family, where do you look for rewards in life? If you search for them in prestige and your career and you don't see your family or friends as rewarding, then there is an emotional tangle in your life that needs sorting out, and it should be sorted out before you seriously try to lose weight. Once you know how much emotion affects your eating, then you can proceed to diet with a good chance of success.

# 3

## THE NEW RELIGION

### Food and Guilt

Are we really what we eat? In the previous chapter we have seen that both overeating and undereating are tied up with our sense of self. The stronger our inner self, the greater control we have over what we eat or don't eat. The weaker that sense is, the less respect we have for ourselves, the more difficult it becomes to control our diet. Curiously, this lack of control, always seems to be tied to a feeling of guilt.

Some researchers in psychology, viewing what has happened to the eating habits of America in the past twenty years, speculate that food has replaced sex as a source of primal guilt. How did it happen?

The United States has been spiraling upward economically. Even with our occasional depressions and recessions, we still lead a richer life than the rest of the world. At this point, over-consumption is a way of life to us. We over-consume on so many levels. We buy more clothes than we need, pleading the vagaries of style to get rid of wearable but outdated apparel. We buy automobiles carelessly, usually for visual rather than mechanical reasons, and we trade them in for new ones long before they are used up. The auto industry has indoctrinated all of us with the firm conviction that there are economic advantages in trading in an automobile every two years.

We replace perfectly good appliances with new ones because the newer ones have a better design or an "in" design. Furniture, rugs, even homes are consumed and overconsumed . . . and of course food is too.

Of all the elements that go to make up our culture, food is the one that we are most involved with. Whether it's on the level of gourmet dining or a fast-food turnover, the variety and number of restaurants we can choose from is overwhelming. We are overconcerned with eating, and overwhelmed by a variety of rich, extravagant foods.

At the same time that we give physical service to overconsumption, we give lip service to the Puritan Ethic; *waste not, want not*. The lesson of frugality is drummed into us all our lives, and we are faced with a strange contradiction between the need for overconsumption to spark the economy on the one hand and deprivation for the good of our souls on the other. Somehow, we are able to believe, as we continue to stuff our stomachs, that a Spartan life of simplicity and temperance is a good one, is in fact an ideal.

The result is our curious association of food and guilt. It's almost as if the symbol of Adam and Eve chomping on the apple has turned eating into the original sin.

We try to assuage the guilt of food in many ways. The current health-food movement has many good things going for it, but it can also be used by many people who suffer from food-guilt as a means of atonement. Scratch a dyed-in-the-wool health-food addict and you're likely to find a good deal of the old-fashioned, hair-shirted, religious fanatic. Many of the more dedicated health-food fanciers seem convinced that the more tasteless the food they eat and the less enjoyable it is, the healthier it has to be, and the better it is for them.

## Healthy, Natural and Organic

At first the nation watched the health-food movement with curiosity. There were only a handful originally, but all at once it seems as if that handful has grown and spread to even the smallest communities. There is hardly a town in the United States that doesn't have a health-food store selling everything from kelp to bran, from soybeans to gluten flour. The selling of health food has become over a billion-dollar-a-year industry, and the word "natural," popularized by the health-food movement, has become a symbol of what is good and wholesome to the entire nation.

Eager to capitalize on this, the big food producers and merchandisers have jumped on the bandwagon, and now every kind of food from breakfast cereal to ice cream and potato chips has "natural" tucked into its labeling and advertising, until the word has become almost meaningless. It's now spread beyond food to soap and hair spray, and I've even seen roach powder advertised as the "Natural Killer."

Along with "natural," "organic" is another byword of the health-food movement. Organically grown food is raised with no chemical sprays or fertilizers, and it is supposed to be much better for us than the less expensive but often prettier products in our supermarkets. To some people, it may well be that the frequently deformed shape and smaller size of the "organic" fruits and vegetables add to their desirability by assuaging their food-guilt. Eating unattractive food can be a way of repenting.

It's an interesting note that Dr. Howard Schneider, the former director of the Institute of Nutrition at the University of North Carolina, has stated that organically grown food is no more nutritious than food sold in regular markets, and the Federal Food and Drug Administration has warned that using the word *health* in connection with foods is misbranding. Such products, the FDA points out, have no more nutritional value than that found in any wholesome food product.

It should also be pointed out, however, that more than nutrition is involved in the increasing popularity of organic foods. Before 1940 almost no chemical fertilizers were used in growing food. Today more than 150 pounds per acre are common, and this does not include insecticides and herbicides. Inevitably these chemicals get into the food chain, are fed into rivers, lakes and the ocean, affect fish and end up in animal feed where they affect animal produce as well. We know of some of the harmful effects of these chemicals, and there may be others we are not aware of. From this view-point, organically grown food, if it is *truly* organic and avoids all insecticides, is less harmful though not necessarily more nutritious.

But even if you decide you want to eat organic food to avoid harmful chemicals, how do you know what you buy in the health-food store is really "organic," even if that's what's on the label? Such labeling is not strictly controlled, and even a sincere health-food store manager has to take the word of his supplier that a product is "organic." The only way to be absolutely sure you are really getting organic food and not getting ripped off is to grow it yourself.


## A Matter of Morality

The interest in health-foods goes hand in hand with a new and almost fanatic devotion to vitamins. They are claimed to cure everything from heart disease to cancer, despite the fact that there is as yet no real scientific consensus on any of these cures. But the very idea of swallowing vitamins (for the vitamin pills resemble medicine) also help many of us assuage the food-guilt syndrome. Medicine is connected with punishment as well as with sickness. "Take your medicine like a man," and of course, punishment expiates guilt.

The greatest way to expiate guilt about food is to deprive yourself of it. And this, perhaps as much as the health or beauty aspect of dieting, is what makes losing weight so popular.

Partial dieting, a diet that omits not only nutritious but tasty food from our meals, is another way of expiating guilt. It seems to me that is what many vegetarians are doing when they eliminate meat from their diets, but of course, one man's meat is another man's poison.

A vegetarian diet can be wholesome and nutritious *if*, and it's an important *if*, you are sure to get enough complete protein. Meat is a complete protein containing all the amino acids, but vegetable proteins are not. You must mix things like rice and beans, peas and rice, or grains with dairy products to make sure you get a complete protein with each meal. If you do this carefully and know what you are doing, a vegetarian diet can be healthy and wholesome, though certainly not to everyone's taste. But many people who don't really know how to maintain a carefully balanced diet (and who also don't care) may embrace vegetarianism as a fad or as a way of assuaging their food-guilt, by denying themselves tasty and healthful food.

Another kind of "morality" involved in vegetarianism is a feeling of horror at the way animals are slaughtered. Upton Sinclair first brought this to the nation's attention in his novel about the Chicago stockyards, *The Jungle*. As a result there was a wave of vegetarianism when the book came out. In our time, with the publication of books like Peter Singer's *Animal Liberation*, vegetarianism is becoming increasingly popular. In fact it almost seems like another aspect of the ideology of nonviolence.

In recent years, this moral aspect of vegetarianism has led to a kind of religious fervor and rebirth, a pseudoreligion that centers around eating.

According to Dr. Sam Keen, who holds a doctorate in philosophy and religion from Princeton University, many people are looking for ways to reestablish a relationship of reverence towards the natural world. In an article in *Psychology Today* (October 1978), Keen says, "Organic gardening, vegetarianism and natural foods are the new sacraments through which the cosmic conscience is reestablished."

## Macrobiotics

Aside from moral and religious aspects of vegetarianism, there is also a firm conviction among many vegetarians that meat is a dangerous food, leading to a wide spectrum of illness—from arthritis to heart disease. The corollary of this idea is the implication that a proper diet, lacking in this or containing that, can cure all ills. This is an extension of the pseudoreligious aspects of vegetarianism. Eat in the way God dictates, and He will cure you. And the enlightened ones will tell you what God dictates!

According to Peggy Taylor, Editor of Boston's *New Age Magazine*, who joined a macrobiotic commune, the connection between religion and diet is very real. Macrobiotics, she believes, is like Christianity. "It's based on the idea that you are not okay, and you have to do something to become okay some time in the future." It contains, Peggy believes, the concept of the fallen man. "When you get down to it, these people believe that food is God, that it is the most important force in your life."

She finally left the commune, but while on her macrobiotic diet, she says that she cheated constantly by gobbling candy bars in secret at every opportunity. Children raised on macrobiotic diets, she insists, feel an almost desperate need for proper protein and calcium, two foods the diet is deficient in. They will sneak milk and cheese whenever they get a chance. "If a macrobiotic kid has been in your house," Peggy warns in another article in the October 1978 issue of *Psychology Today*, "look in the refrigerator and there will be teethmarks in the cheese!''

The "religious" aspect of dieting goes beyond the overconsumption-guilt syndrome. There is also an element of confession to the process. Taking off weight is a punishment, but it is also an absolution for the sin of gluttony. You have confessed to your sin, and you have taken the punishment of a diet. What follows is the absolution of the weight loss. You come out of it all a new, slimmer person, reborn in a different body, and of course you now have the freedom to go forth and sin again, forget the diet and gorge on all the rich and tasty foods you can reach. After all, confession and absolution are always available. Diets are a dime a dozen. Another diet, another punishment, and you can be a born-again glutton!

In discussing macrobiotics and other aspects of vegetarianism, I may have given the impression that all vegetarian diets are a bit off-base. This is far from true. Even the early stages of the macrobiotic diet is well-balanced and sensible. It is partly the fervor and hoopla, the religious intensity that go with the diet that I object to. And in the higher stages of macrobiotics, I also object to the lack of protein. This lack of proper protein can be a serious problem with any vegetarian diet.

I became very aware of this at the recent wedding of two friends, Jill and Larry. They are both deeply committed people, committed to saving the environment, banning nuclear power, helping the whales survive and the fight for feminist rights. When they decided to get married at the country home of a close friend, the feminist issue became intrusive in an unusual way.

Looking about for a catering service, they found one that operated locally and came well-recommended. "What kind of food will they serve?" Jill's mother asked as she made out the check for the caterer.

"Veggies," Jill said vaguely. "We left it up to them. They're total vegetarians."

"But darling . . . total?" Jill's mother was dismayed thinking of the sensitive digestive tracts of some of her older friends. "Not even a ham or a turkey?"

"All veggies." Seeing her mother's stricken look, Jill explained, "It's all their conscience allows them to serve."

"There are other catering services . . . "

"We just had to have this group do it, Mom. They're very deserving, a feminist catering service, and they need every job they can get."

At the wedding dinner, Jill's mother sat down at our table with a plate heaped with Bulghur salad, curried brown rice, four different bean appetizers, vegetable barley, and so on and so forth. She stared down at it all in a stunned way, murmuring, "My God! I'll never be the same."

We ate uneasily, quickly filled by the vast quantity of bulk, and suffered with the after-effects of the meal for the next few days.

Our systems weren't used to the bulk, and even if they were, the absence of animal protein would have troubled us—especially if we had remained on such a diet for any considerable time. The buffet table that Jill's friends prepared was suspiciously like one of the later stages of the macrobiotic diet.

## The Yang and Yin of It

So many of us have heard of the macrobiotic diet and so much has been written about it, good and bad, that it is important to explain just what it is. Macrobiotics is the creation of George Ohsawa, a philosopher and teacher. He began teaching macrobiotics in 1953 in India. Then three years later, he gave Europe the benefit of his philosophy on a grand tour. He established a macrobiotic factory in Belgium and macrobiotic stores and restaurants throughout the continent, turning it into a profitable industry.

In 1960 his foundation published *Zen Macrobiotics* and also started a magazine in New York City, first called *The Macrobiotic News* and later *The Macrobiotic* when he moved his base to California, the land of cults and sunshine.

The first American macrobiotic food manufacturing and distributing company was founded by a group of thirteen families of Ohsawa disciples in Chico, California. Ohsawa is reported to have advised Mao Tse-tung about his health and the problems of China. As a philosophy and way of life, macrobiotics is based rather loosely on Buddhist symbolism and manifestations of the yang and yin principles.

In his book, *The Unique Principle,* Ohsawa said that *Yang* and *Yin* "has an organic mechanism invisible to mechanical researchers. It is like the 'flying arrow,' out of reach of those who want to possess it through analysis." The point he's after is that once you grasp hold of the flying arrow, it is no longer flying. While to some this seems a great philosophical truth, to others it seems a self-evident cop-out, a great excuse for not trying to explain a process.

His yang and yin philosophy states that the universe is composed of the movement of two basic forces, yang and yin, male and female, contraction and expansion, animal and vegetable, fire and water and so on down to bitter, salty opposed to sweet, sour.

When these principles interact, Ohsawa declares, "it can produce itself at all levels, be it the depths of the sea or on a high plateau—of necessity assuming different forms according to the milieu and the time—because any being is its transformed environment, no being existing independently of its surroundings."

The philosophy of Ohsawa, if you can wash it free of its muddy prose, poses questions about being, knowledge, self and free will; its disciples apply it to chemistry and biology, and from this, to an analysis of vegetarianism. Here yin consists of acidity and yang alkalinity. The basic principle behind the macrobiotic diet calls for a balance of these two elements in the body and attempts to create such a balance with different foods. Macrobiotic philosophy claims that man is the result of his environment and can maintain perfect health only if he eats foods that are in his environment "in the very same proportions that they are naturally produced." Too much yang, or too much yin and you're in big trouble, out of balance—sick.

Every sickness, Ohsawa says, is caused by such an imbalance, and he has set forth an elaborate dieting scheme that lists various stages to go through to achieve perfection. The lowest stage, the one you start the diet with, allows you 10 percent cereals, 30 percent vegetables, 10 percent

57

soup, 30 percent animal products, 15 percent fruit and salad and 5 percent desserts.

From this you proceed upward in ten stages to the ultimate diet that includes 100 percent brown rice and only eight ounces of fluid a day. Every bite of food you take into your mouth on this diet must be chewed fifty times.

The first stage of the macrobiotic diet is not too harmful. In fact, it can be a very healthful diet and bears a strong resemblance to a modified form of vegetarianism. But the tenth stage is dangerously deficient in complete protein. Enough protein to satisfy any dietary needs can be gotten from certain vegetable products, but the most complete protein, in terms of human needs, comes from the animal, not the vegetable world.

Grazing animals are magnificent machines for turning plant life into animal protein, and the animal protein we eat most in the United States is beef. Now vegetarianism, when it is isolated from the philosophy of macrobiotics and the other semi-religious cults that surround it, has a great deal going for it. But before we go into that, let's consider beef, the food vegetarians love to hate.

# 4

## GUILTY FOODS

### Why Beef?

One of the foods that Americans eat in abundance
without feeling any pangs of guilt is beef. (The
other is sugar, and more about that later.) Our
national indulgence in beef is in direct contrast to
the self-denial of small groups such as those who
favor a macrobiotic diet. Martin and his family are
typical beef overindulgers.

"Let's go out to eat," Martin says to his wife
after one look around the living room. The two
kids have made a shambles of it. Eve looks dis-
traught, her clothes disheveled, hair clinging to her
damp face. She was trying to straighten up, a
hopeless task unless she could hypnotize the kids
with TV. But it was still too early for their
program. "You deserve a break today," Martin
adds, singing it out in McDonald's fashion.

"Let's go, let's go!" the children chorus, as Eve
draws a sigh of relief.

"I really could use a break," Eve sighed. "Let
me change my blouse, and I'll be right along. You
kids get out to the car."

And America's "typical" family is off to
McDonalds, or Burger King, or Wendy's or any
one of the dozens of hamburger houses that have
sprung up, some say like a blight, all over the face
of our land.

The hamburger, belying its name because it has

no ham in it, is the most popular of America's fast foods and continues to account for the fact that in spite of the growing popularity of vegetarianism, the average American eats more than a hundred pounds of beef a year.

The typical businessman relaxes in a hotel dining room after a tough day on the road by ordering a juicy steak and all the trimmings. Dad takes mother out for a very special Sunday dinner (no fast food this time) and orders prime ribs, red and rare. When the boss comes to dinner a roast beef is a fool-proof production with a touch of prestige, and every summer Sunday, the crackle of the charcoal grill is heard in the backyard as hamburgers char over the coals.

It is only in recent years, and probably because of the upsurge of fast-food hamburger chains, that beef has become the most popular meat in our country. In 1950, pork was still the leader in the race. Ten years later, beef was ahead. In 1970 it became a front runner, and now, by the eighties, twice as much beef is consumed.

In the 1800s, pork was the great meat staple in the United States, but once the West was opened, the new grazing lands made it cheaper to produce beef. Refrigeration and quick transportation solved the problem of getting the meat back East and changed Chicago from the "Hog Butcher of the World" to a major beef-producing city.

In the early days of beef production, the vast grasslands provided cheap, easy fodder for grazing cattle. But as civilization spread westward, so did farming. The grazing land became scarcer and more expensive, and eventually it grew more economical to stock-raise cattle. The hardy longhorns which were so good on the open range were replaced with the more tender Herefords. Corn, alfalfa, soybeans and a variety of grains were used to fatten the cattle while they were kept penned up. Eventually, vitamins and hormones, added to the feed, speeded up the process. Because the feed was so rich, the cattle so inactive and the hormone doses so massive, the meat produced was no longer lean as it had been when cattle were raised on the range. Beef began to appear marbled with fat, and of course, as it was cooked, the fat made it tender and soft. This was the most desirable beef, labeled *prime*.

All of these factors have helped to make beef into America's favorite food. But of all of them, the most potent is probably the roadside hamburger chain. So much beef is consumed in these quickie restaurants that outfits like McDonald's have their own herds of cattle and control the entire process of hamburger production.

## The Problem With Beef

Is beef so terrible for us? Just what is there about beef that raises the hackles of vegetarians and doctors? Is a diet heavy in beef really unhealthy? Don't we need the animal protein it gives us?

There are two main problems with beef, and some advantages. As we said before, it is an excellent source of protein. Unfortunately, it is also an excellent source of fat. Even in lean beef, one third of the calories come from the fat. It's almost impossible to produce fat-free beef—at least if we want to keep it edible.

61

We've now mentioned the ubiquitous word *calorie*, without which no book about dieting could be written and hardly any diet could be planned. Pay no attention to the specialists who tell you that calories don't count. They damned well do, and your first job is to understand just what a calorie is. A calorie is the amount of heat needed to raise one gram of water one degree centigrade at sea level. It is also—and this is how it is used here and in other books on dieting—a unit that expresses the energy released when food is burned up by the body. We speak of food having, say, sixty calories to an ounce when one ounce provides sixty calories of heat, or more properly, of energy.

The importance of calories in dieting will be considered a bit later, but to get back to meat, the prime problem (and the problem with prime) is the amount of fat in beef. In cheap hamburger meat at the supermarket it can be as high as one-half. In lean beef it is one-third of the total. In the more expensive prime beef, the proportion is higher, and of course so is the caloric content. Fat is a great source of calories.

The second problem with beef and other meats, lamb, veal, and pork, is the type of fat it contains. Most of the fat in beef is *saturated* fat. There is a little *polyunsaturated* fat and a good deal of *monounsaturated* fat, and this brings us to saturated and unsaturated fats and their advantages and disadvantages.

To understand saturation, take a glass of water and start adding salt or sugar, stirring until it is dissolved. There will come a point when no more sugar or salt will dissolve in the water. The water is now a saturated solution. In a similar fashion, a molecule of fat holds a lot of hydrogen atoms. If it holds all the hydrogen atoms it can, it is considered saturated. When two more hydrogen atoms can be added, the fat is called *monounsaturated*. If more than two atoms can be added, it's *polyunsaturated*. Usually, unsaturated fats turn liquid at room temperatures.

Dairy products, such as butter, are also composed of saturated fats. Margarine, offered as an unsaturated substitute for butter, is a liquid in its unsaturated form. Since no one likes to spread a liquid on bread, margarine must be hardened, and hardening it also saturates it. Saturating means adding hydrogen atoms, and the label tells us this by using the word hydrogenated. Most of us are unaware that hydrogenation consists of saturating the unsaturated margarine!

To give you an idea of the proportions of polyunsaturated fats, saturated fats and monounsaturated fats in some common foods, consider the following table, adapted from Dr. Lawrence E. Lamb's book, *What You Need to Know About Food and Cooking For Health*.

| 100 grams of: | Calories of polyunsaturated fats | Calories of monounsaturated fats | Calories of saturated fats |
|---|---|---|---|
| Lean beef (round steak) | 2 | 49 | 54 |
| T-bone steak | 7 | 148 | 162 |
| Hamburger | 4 | 84 | 93 |
| Bluefish | 10 | 10 | 9 |
| Trout | 6 | 6 | 5 |
| Chicken | 9 | 17 | 15 |
| Peanuts | 117 | 167 | 84 |
| Swiss cheese | 9 | 79 | 132 |
| 2 eggs (100 gms) | 18 | 80 | 72 |
| Vegetables | | only traces | |
| Fruits | | only traces | |

Beef and dairy products such as butter and cheese are highest in saturated fats, but just how does all this affect our health? How do we react to these fats and which, if any, are better for us?

Long-term cardiac studies have found that replacing the saturated fat in a diet with poly-unsaturated fat has led to a decrease in heart attacks. This may be because polyunsaturated fats seem to have a cholesterol-lowering effect. Just how this happens is not too clear, but a kind of deductive reasoning has convinced researchers that it is true. For example, populations who have little signs of arteriosclerosis and high blood pressure, conditions that can lead to heart disease, usually have diets high in polyunsaturated fats.

People in cultures who have high rates of heart attacks usually have a diet high in saturated fats. Now this is presumptive evidence, but it's enough to make us think twice about the quality of our diet. Of course there are other factors involved—obesity, stress, inactivity, smoking—all of these increase your chances of a heart attack.

### The Good and the Bad of Cholesterol

Another substance in our bodies that seems closely associated with heart disease is cholesterol. Cholesterol looks like a fat because it's a solid, waxy substance, but chemically it's an alcohol. It occurs in many parts of our bodies, and we need it. It's an essential ingredient in forming hormones and nerve tissue. We wouldn't have a brain without cholesterol. Cholesterol is an animal product not found in the vegetable kingdom, but there's a lot of it in organ meats and egg yolks, and a moderate amount of it in shellfish.

Cholesterol occurs in the bile formed by our liver, and it spills into the small intestine. Here it mixes with the cholesterol that we eat, and a part of it is absorbed by the body to enter the bloodstream. Now how much cholesterol we have in our blood depends on more than how much cholesterol we eat. If we eat a lot of saturated fat we seem to produce a lot of cholesterol, more than we need.

There is a good deal of talk about cholesterol blood levels. Well, a blood level of 200 milligrams or less is pretty safe. If our blood level is above 240, our risk of a heart attack is increased. Just why this happens is a bit uncertain, but how it happens is clear. Cholesterol and fat can be deposited on the inner walls of our blood vessels, narrowing them and sometimes closing them off. This is the condition called arteriosclerosis. Narrowing the arteries means that less blood is going to reach the tissues, less oxygen and food. When this happens to heart tissue, we have a heart attack.

There is a great deal of controversy about how much cholesterol is healthy in our diet, and every once in a while someone will declare that cutting back our cholesterol intake is silly and does us no good. The U.S. Department of Agriculture and the U.S. Department of Health, Education and Welfare think differently. In February 1980 they declared, "For the United States population as a whole, reduction in our intake of cholesterol is sensible. This suggestion is particularly appropriate for people who have high blood pressure or who smoke."

They go on to say that there is no reason to prohibit any special food or not to eat a variety of fats.

"For example," they explain, "eggs and organ meats such as liver contain cholesterol, but they also contain many essential vitamins and minerals as well. Such items can be eaten in moderation as long as your overall cholesterol intake is not excessive."

To get an idea of how much cholesterol different foods contain, consider this list.

| 100 grams of | Cholesterol content |
| --- | --- |
| Brains | more than 2,000 mgs. |
| Eggs (2) | 550 |
| Kidney | 375 |
| Liver | 300 |
| Butter (8 tablespoons) | 250 |
| Lobster | 200 |
| Cream cheese | 120 |
| Cheddar cheese | 100 |
| Fish | 70 |
| Beef | 70 |
| Ice cream | 45 |
| Milk | 11 |

So far we have considered two aspects of beef that can be held against it as a food. One is its high fat content; another is the fact that its fat is saturated. A high intake of saturated fat and cholesterol together, researchers have found, can increase blood cholesterol levels in most people.

It is true that individual physiologies vary a great deal and some people can eat as much saturated fat and cholesterol as they want and still have normal blood-cholesterol levels; a few others will have high blood-cholesterol levels even when they go on a low-fat, low-cholesterol diet. But most people react with lower blood levels of cholesterol when cholesterol and saturated fats are kept out of their diet. Another point to remember is that children should rarely, if ever, have their cholesterol restricted. They need it to grow on.

A third reason to look on beef with suspicion is the additive problem. In the United States, beef is often loaded with harmful substances. There is diethylstilbestrol, an artificial hormone fed to cattle to make them mature quickly and to soften their meat. There are residues of DDT and other pesticides in cattle feed as well as antibiotics.

All of this should make us think twice before chomping down on that hamburger. Meat may still be a good source of protein, especially if you don't have to watch calories and haven't a cholesterol problem. But you should be a bit concerned about all those additives.

If you want to lose weight, however, and you decide to limit your fat consumption, there are ways of getting the most protein and the least fat out of your meat. First of all, trim it thoroughly before cooking. Remember that the leaner cuts are better for you even if they are chewier, and the lower grades of meat, choice rather than prime, are better because they have less fat. Round steak is a lean cut, and so is flank steak. Hamburger can be very high in fat—two-thirds of the commercial hamburger is fat—unless you grind it yourself. And finally, if in spite of everything you are a confirmed beef eater, stick to a quarter pound a day. This won't do too much harm.

## How Sweet It Is

All the evils of beef fade away in the face of a far greater evil, sugar—at least according to the "mavens" of the diet world—and they may well be correct. Sugar is surely the most ubiquitous of all foods. It crops up everywhere. Start reading the labels on the common foods in your pantry, and you'll find that some degree of sugar is contained in almost every one. Only recently has sugar been taken out of baby food, but it still remains in peanut butter, spaghetti sauce, canned spaghetti and ravioli, canned meats and chicken, tomato soup, salad dressings (even low-calorie ones), mayonnaise, ketchup, breakfast cereals, canned fruits, white bread, tomato juice, any fruit drink labeled punch or cocktail, canned sweet peas, canned succotash, corn and kidney beans.

Most brands of applesauce have it unless it says there is none on the label, but to my surprise, in a recent check of my local supermarket's shelves, I found a brand of applesauce labeled "unsweetened with corn sweetener added." In that same check I found sugar in foods where I would never expect to find it—in hot dogs, sausages, and I know it's in most fast-food hamburgers and fried chicken. The list seems endless. When you do your next shopping, read the food labels carefully, remembering that manufacturers will often disguise sugar by calling it corn sweetener. The order of the ingredients listed on the label, and most foods must list them by law, tells how much of each ingredient is in it. If sugar is listed first, *most* of the food is sugar. Check out chocolate, cocoa or Ovaltine mixes. Believe it or not, sugar is the first ingredient.

We are a nation of sugar eaters; some say we are

addicted to it, and not only in the candy bars we munch on, or the ice cream cones, or sweet desserts —the most obvious sources of sugar—but also in the less obvious sources: the sugar added to just about every food on the supermarket shelf.

And all this sugar has a serious effect on our health. There has been enough research done to convince scientists that an excessive amount of granulated sugar is a major factor in causing heart and vascular disease.

It is an obvious fact in dental circles that refined sugar is a primary cause of dental decay. Instead of the television commercial urging toothpastes with fluoride to combat tooth decay, why not a commercial urging us to avoid sugar. It wouldn't sell toothpaste, but it would help our teeth. And the next time you buy toothpaste, especially for your children, make sure it doesn't contain sugar. Some brands do!

Another problem with all the sugar we're fed is the strong possibility that it can cause a form of diabetes, a dangerous, disabling disease. That sugar is a probable cause of diabetes is strengthened by the fact that during World Wars I and II, when sugar was extremely scarce, the incidence of diabetes and the number of deaths due to it declined dramatically. Another link between sugar and diabetes is the rarity of diabetes in societies that do not use refined sugar.

All of these are good reasons to avoid refined sugar in your diet, or at least to cut down on the amount of sugar you do eat. On an *average*, we consume about 150 pounds of sugar per person in the United States each year. But another very good reason to cut down on sugar is the high caloric content of the stuff. A quarter of a pound of chicken contains about 100 calories, while a quarter pound of sugar has 400 calories, and if ever a food was crammed full of empty calories, sugar is it. Nutritionally, sugar adds nothing to a diet, no vitamins, no fats, no proteins—just the wrong kind of carbohydrates.


## The Many Faces of Carbohydrates

What are carbohydrates? All of the food that we eat and use to grow, develop and stay alive, can be broken down into a small number of categories. There are the inorganic elements, the minerals such as iron, phosphorus and calcium. These are essential to our health and so are the organic parts of our diet. Vitamins are organic, and so are the larger categories of food, *proteins, fats,* and *carbohydrates.*

Carbohydrates exist in different forms, and sugar is one. There are many kinds of sugars. Refined sugar is sucrose, not a very desirable kind. This is the sugar that goes into most of our foods. Starch is another carbohydrate. These two, starch and sugar, are the forms of carbohydrates that we can handle. Both starch and sugar are changed into glucose in our bodies. Glucose is the sugar we use as fuel to drive our bodies. It is the source of all our energy. Our system uses glucose by breaking it down into carbon dioxide and water, and in the process, energy is released. It's this energy that's the breath of life.

Some foods, fruit and certain vegetables, contain glucose as a carbohydrate. Other foods, grain cereals and vegetables, contain starch as a carbohydrate. There are also some amounts of carbohydrates in many other foods.

If the carbohydrates in our diet come from vegetables, fruits and grain cereals, a great deal of bulk goes along with them, and so do vitamins and minerals. Bulk, vitamins, minerals are all necessary to our health.

If the carbohydrates are processed and turned into refined sugar, sucrose, they give us far more energy than we can use, and that excess is stored in our bodies as fat. Sugar is a quick and sure road to obesity.

## The Body's Building Blocks

While carbohydrates give us the energy we need to get up and go, proteins give us the material to go with. Our bodies are constructed out of protein—muscle, bone, blood and skin—all except the fat is protein. Children need plenty of protein because they are in the process of building up their bodies, but adults also need it to replace their worn-out parts.

Protein is made up of units like building blocks, units called amino acids. Most of these acids can be manufactured by the body from sugar or fat, but there are some our bodies cannot make. We call these the essential amino acids, and we must get them from the food we eat.

When times grow lean and no food is available, our bodies will break down their stored fat and turn it into energy. Once the fat in our bodies is used up, we turn to the protein and use that to survive. When this happens, in starvation, our muscles gradually waste away.

When starvation is no threat and food is plentiful, we get our essential amino acids from meat—beef, lamb, pork, poultry and fish—and we get some from dairy products, such as milk and cheese. Some grain cereals, nuts and vegetables also yield proteins, but these proteins, unlike animal proteins, are usually free of fat, one of the reasons that vegetarians tend to be thin.

It is difficult, but not impossible, to get all of your essential amino acids from a vegetarian diet. If you combine vegetables with some dairy products, it's much easier. Adding milk, eggs or cheese to rice, wheat, corn, soybeans or peanuts gives you all the necessary amino acids to build protein. If you are a total vegetarian and can't abide any dairy products, you can still come up with sufficient dietary protein from vegetables alone. It does, however, take a bit of juggling and combining. According to Frances Moore Lappé, mixing legumes (peas and beans) with rice will do it. So will soybeans mixed with rice and wheat, or beans mixed with wheat. If you wish to use nuts and seeds, soybeans, peanuts and sesame seeds will cover the necessary amino acid spectrum, and so will soybeans, peanuts, wheat and rice, or soybeans, sesame and wheat. With all these combinations, the body can manufacture protein.

If you opt for fresh vegetables, you can mix and match them with sesame seeds and brazil nuts, millet, converted rice or mushrooms. These could all help round out your total amino acid needs so that the body can build protein.


## A Balanced Diet

Between the self-denial of diets like the macrobiotic one and the self-indulgence of excess sugar and beef, there must be a commonsense middle road. This is the well-balanced diet.

We've considered the important basic types of food. The next consideration is how much of each type should make up a balanced diet that is nutritionally sound. To get along without gaining or losing weight, a normal sedentary person uses up roughly 2,500 calories a day. Some use more, some less. Women usually use less, but let's work with 2,500 as an example. With this as a base, we'll let Mr. or Mrs. Sedentary take in 2,500 calories in food. How should this food be broken up? How much protein? How much fat and how much carbohydrate should he or she eat in the course of a day?

While there are no rigid rules for this sort of thing, about 280 to 300 of the calories should be protein. This is more than enough even for a growing child.

There's bound to be some fat in any diet, but heart specialists suggest that fat should be limited to less than 35 percent of all the calories. For the 2,500 calorie diet, this would come to around 875 calories. Of this fat, at least one third should be polyunsaturated. No more than one third should be saturated, and the rest should be monounsaturated.

With 280 calories of protein and 875 of fat, our sedentary citizen should add about 1,220 calories of carbohydrates. The remaining calories can be a dab of that dubious alcohol, cholesterol. These proportions will allow you to live in nutritional comfort. If you choose the right foods out of these categories, you won't need any vitamins, nor will you gain or lose weight if you continue to be moderately sedentary.

# 5

## THE TROUBLE WITH DIETS

### Evelyn and the Yo-Yo Effect

In spite of the fact that a well-balanced diet is common sense and all the foods that go into it are available in this country, Americans in general seem unable to follow it. We have love affairs with all kinds of diets, the kooky and the dangerous, the faddish and the idiotic, but somehow we seem unable to settle down with the right one. There is a thriving diet book industry out there, but people still stay fat. Take my wife's friend, Evelyn.

Evelyn, my wife, Barbara, and I were sitting on the ledge of the pool after a tough workout in the health club gym, when one of the overweight women said, "An hour's workout and twenty minutes in the steam room has to take it off."

"Take what off?" A thin, athletic type paused in her knee bends long enough to ask.

"My ten extra pounds. I've got to lose them for the weekend. We've got a wedding coming up, and I don't fit into my gown."

Evelyn, her face glistening with sweat, said, "Diet! It's the only answer. Steam will never do it. All the weight you lose in there is only water."

Looking at Evelyn doubtfully, one of the overweight women asked, "You ever dieted?"

"You've looking at a real diet bum. I have tried every diet ever conceived," Evelyn told us, "and each one works. I think losing weight is very easy.

Hell, I've done it so often." She frowned. "In fact, I once added up all the weight I ever lost, and it came to 500 pounds. Isn't that fantastic?"

I looked at Evelyn's ample middle-aged girth straining the swimsuit that wrapped her, at her heavy arms and enormous thighs, her apple cheeks and jowls, and I shook my head. "Evelyn, if you've lost five hundred pounds, why is it you're still more than a hundred pounds overweight?"

"That's what I'd like to know," she sighed, wiping the sweat from her face. "I try. I really do. Now take Dr. Taller's diet. I stuck with that faithfully for six months."

"What happened?" the athletic one asked.

"I lost close to fifty pounds pretty quickly. I really felt I was on the way to success."

"And then?"

Evelyn shrugged. "I went for my yearly medical exam and the doctor was delighted. He's always after me to lose weight, but when my blood tests came back he made me go off the diet. My cholesterol was too high. Another thing, the diet got me into the habit of six meals a day, small meals, but when I went off the diet I stayed on the six-a-day routine, only I ate regular meals. I bounced up again, like a yo-yo!"

After that talk with Evelyn at the health club I checked out the Taller high-protein, low-carbohydrate diet. The current prophet for the diet is Dr. Carlton Fredericks, a popular nutritionist who has been on the radio for nearly a quarter of a century and has written a number of books on nutrition.

Dr. Fredericks' reworking of the Taller diet (publicized in Dr. Herman Taller's book *Calories Don't Count*) is based on the conclusion that all people are different in terms of how they oxidize or

75

burn up food. This is one of the reasons he questions the importance of calories, and like Dr. Taller, says they don't count.

Put out now as a low-carbohydrate diet, Fredericks' book *Dr. Carlton Fredericks' Low-Carbohydrate Diet,* advises, "1. The diet should be low in starch and sugar. 2. It should be high in protein. 3. It should be moderately high in fat. 4. About a fifth of this fat should be polyunsaturated for that will help in the burning of body fat. 5. Experience teaches that such a diet need not be restrictive in calories. 6. The diet should be fed in at least six meals (not snacks) daily." It also restricts salt and suggests vitamins C and E.

I took a copy of the low-carbohydrate diet to Beverly Daniel, a public health nutritionist and a close friend. Beverly has taught nutrition for many years, so I felt secure in asking her how effective Dr. Fredericks' diet was.

"Effective? It certainly may take off weight," she told me. "For a lot of people it's a comfortable and rapid way to lose pounds."

I told her about my wife's friend, Evelyn. "She said she had to go off it eventually because of her cholesterol, and yet the book I read on the diet says it lowers blood cholesterol."

"I think Evelyn's experience is more typical. This type of diet has been around for a while. It's not that new, and we've found that if you stay on it for a long time, your blood cholesterol *can* go up. You see, in addition to the fat in the diet, you're taking in a great deal of animal protein, and animal protein contains saturated fat. The diet suggests beef, pork and eggs. They all contain saturated fat and cholesterol. Logically, that *should* increase your blood cholesterol level. I guess it's an effective diet, but I'd stay on it only a short while, a few weeks maybe. It has the psychological advantage of a good steak as a reward for dieting, and all clean-cut Americans want to be rewarded with a steak dinner for doing good. This diet gives it to you. Also, all that meat gives you a sense of fullness. You *feel* full, not hungry."

"Who wouldn't on six meals a day?"

Beverly shrugged. "Well, they're not very big meals, though the original Taller diet said you could eat all the meat and fats you wanted. That always bothered me."

"Even on Dr. Fredericks' version of the diet," I said, "it seems to me that things like deviled eggs, cream sauce, avocados, pork chops, mayonnaise and candy—all the things he allows—are very high in calories.

"Very high and full of cholesterol," she replied, "but then his claim is that calories don't count."

I asked another friend, Dr. Amy Gelfand, who is assistant clinical instructor in family medicine at University Hospital in Stony Brook, New York, what she thought of the low-carbohydrate, high-protein diet, and she threw up her hands. "I hate fad diets! Oh hell, for a week or two I guess they're all right, providing you go back to normal eating afterwards."

"But is the diet safe?" I asked.

"I think it's potentially dangerous. It seems to me all that protein puts a strain on your system. It's just not my idea of a sensible way to lose weight." She shook her head thoughtfully. "There's another thing that bothers me about this current craze for high-protein diets. They can interfere with calcium absorption. Studies have shown they reduce the amount of calcium absorbed by the body, and in older people, women particularly, it's very important to keep from losing calcium.''

''Most dieters are women.''

''Yes, and women, especially after menopause, are particularly susceptible to calcium loss. The bones become weak and break easily, and as the spine weakens they get that dowager's hump look.'' She sighed. ''I just wish people would eat sensibly and not have to diet.''


## Water, Water Everywhere

The next time Evelyn came out of the pool, her bathing suit seemed as tight as ever, and her huge bulk seemed just as massive. I told her about my friend's reaction to her diet, and she shook her head as she eased herself down. ''What I'm into now is fantastic, a real punishment!''

''What is it called?'' Our thin, athletic friend had joined us, and she seemed amused.

''It's Dr. Stillman's diet, or the water diet. That's what one of my friends calls it. She has a weight problem too, and she lost twenty pounds on it.''

''Well, tell us about it.'' A few of our friends moved in closer to listen.

''First of all,'' Evelyn said, ''you have to drink a lot of water.''

''That's good. I know water's healthy. I have at least two glasses a day.''

''Two glasses!'' Evelyn sneered. ''Hey, this diet makes you drink at *least* eight glasses of water a day, even more if you can. A half a glass every hour. It's like the water washes the fat away. It really washes away the ashes of the burnt-up fat.''

Evelyn went on to outline the water diet. She could eat lean meats, beef, lamb, veal, chicken, turkey, all lean fish, eggs, cottage cheese, farmer's cheese, pot cheese, but no butter, margarine, oil or any other kind of fat. In short, it attempted to be an all-protein diet, no fat, no carbohydrate, no alcohol, just protein and water!

"All that water must make you run to the john pretty often," Barbara's athletic friend said.

Evelyn adjusted her towel suspiciously, "It does. So what?"

"Well, I think that much exercise alone would take off weight."

When I left the gym that night, I wondered about Evelyn's new diet. On it, according to Dr. Stillman, in his *Doctor's Quick Inches-Off Diet,* "You may eat as much as you want, without stuffing yourself, of the all protein foods listed—and no other foods while you're on the diet."

I asked Beverly Daniel, my dietician friend, about the Stillman diet, and she shrugged. "What can I say? Sure, it may take off weight. Any diet that eliminates carbohydrates and fats will take off weight, but I hate to think of what it can do to your body."

"What it can do," Dr. Gelfand explained when I asked her about the Stillman diet, "is play hell with your electrolyte balance."

"What's that?"

"To make it very simple, there's a balance in your body between acids and bases. With this all-protein diet, the balance can easily be thrown off and your body can become too acidic. Sure, the diet advocates a lot of water, not to wash away the burnt ashes of the fats, but to wash out the poisons

79

created by the diet. Our kidneys excrete the breakdown products of protein metabolism. They'll be working day and night on this diet. Also, I just don't see depriving your system of bulk, and the greatest sources of bulk are vegetables and fruit.''

A few weeks after that, a bunch of us from the gym went out for coffee afterwards. Evelyn decided she would have apple pie a-la-mode with hers. "You can add an extra dollop of ice cream," she told the waitress. "They've got this fantastic Bassett's ice cream here," she confided, trying to get comfortable in the booth and not quite making it. "It has to be the greatest."

"Ice cream *and* pie? I said. What happened to the protein and water?"

"Oh, I quit that diet," Evelyn said. "No bulk," she added sadly. "A lot of weight came off fast, but moving my bowels, if I may go into an indelicate subject, was a drag. I got into the suppository habit and then started with enemas . . . ''

"Spare us," our athletic friend shuddered. "So you went off it, but you don't look as if you're any thinner. I thought you said the diet took off a lot of weight."

"And so it did, so it did, but it was all those no-no foods that did me in, and put it all back."

"No-no foods?"

"There was a list of foods that were no-nos, like all rich desserts, pasta, candy, Brie cheese—God, how I love Brie cheese—alcohol; they were all no-nos, so of course I went off the diet and gobbled up all I could get my hands on. I was like a prisoner suddenly turned loose. Can an ex-con ever get enough freedom? How could I get enough ice cream or pie or candy? It was fantastic—and of course all the weight came back on. The old yo-yo effect," she said in a sad voice, but with eager eyes, as she dug into her pie and ice cream.

"But fruits and vegetables were no-nos on the diet. Didn't you pig out on them afterwards?"

She shook her head pityingly. "None of you seem to understand the psychology of fat. There isn't a chubby who enjoys fruits or vegetables. That's one of the things that made the water diet bearable in the first place. I didn't have to eat fruits, vegetables or those cruddy salads. I ate real food." Wistfully, she added, "I'm thinking of going back on the diet for a few weeks. You've no idea how good all these rich foods taste afterwards."

### Slathering Mayonnaise

"I have just finished a fabulous book," Evelyn later told me with excited glee the next time we met on our way to the gym. "It's by Dr. Atkins, and it's all about his new diet. I'm going to start it next week."

"The book?"

"No, stupid. The diet, and what a diet! It's going to allow me to slather mayonnaise on my cold salmon, to quote the good doctor who invented it. I'll be able to put butter sauce on my lobster and asparagus and crunch away on fried pork rinds, stuffed olives, gourmet cheese, caviar, deviled eggs—I'm going to live it up on this diet— and watch the weight melt away."

81

"But it doesn't sound like a diet," one of the other stout women protested.

"It is. It just allows me some great food. After the first week I can have bacon and eggs or ham and eggs for breakfast, even steak, and heavy cream in my coffee!"

Pressing Evelyn for further information, I found that during the first week of the diet she could eat any amount of any meat, as long as it didn't have fillers (no sausage or hotdogs) any fowl, but no stuffing, any fish except shellfish, eggs, butter, mayonnaise, cheese and four teaspoons of heavy cream a day.

As in the other diets, Evelyn was admonished to forget calories and eat as much food as she wanted. Unlike the Stillman diet, the Atkins diet doesn't force water. According to Dr. Atkins, in his *Dr. Atkins' Diet Revolution*, you are allowed "steak plus almost any meat, fish or fowl . . . including such usually forbidden goodies as ham, spareribs, bacon, roast pork, corned beef, roast duck, lobster with butter sauce."

What it boils down to is a heavy protein diet with a good deal of fat, but as little carbohydrate as possible. Bread, cake, candy, ice cream, rice, pastry are all forbidden. The best part of the diet, according to Evelyn, is the huge amount you can eat. "The more you eat, the more you lose," she insisted.

According to Dr. Atkins, the lack of carbohydrates doesn't allow the food you eat to be stored as fat. It's metabolized and excreted. The excretion of ketones in the urine, Atkins stresses, is the way you know the diet is working, and he recommends using test strips to check your urine daily.

When we saw Evelyn a few months later, however, she seemed as heavy as ever. How did the diet go? She shook her head sadly. "I didn't lose on it. In fact, I gained," she said woefully. Then she brightened up. "On the other hand, I had a ball eating all those foods, and you know," she gave an embarrassed grin, "I'm starting a new, sure-fire diet . . . "

My medical friend, Dr. Gelfand, laughed when I told her of Evelyn's experience. "Most people do gain weight on a high-calorie diet," she said. "Why do you find that surprising?"

"But what about Dr. Atkins' theory about burning up the fat when carbohydrates are missing?"

"I don't know about that," she shrugged. "His system doesn't fit in with what I've been taught, but new theories of nutrition surface every day. Your fat friend was probably eating close to 5,000 calories a day. You might lose weight on that kind of a diet, but I doubt it. The chances are you'll gain weight. I just find it hard to believe that restricting carbohydrates alone will take off weight, even though I've read some reports that suggest it does happen. It's my belief that you have to restrict your total caloric intake as well. The body can convert fats into glucose for fuel even if no carbohydrates are available." She hesitated. "What bothers me about the Atkins diet is the possibility of harm to the kidneys and the definite disturbance of the electrolyte balance and the pH of the blood. Why can't your friend simply go on an old-fashioned, low-calorie diet?"

"I'll ask her," I said, and the next time I saw Evelyn I asked, "Haven't you had enough of fad diets?"

"I think I've finally latched onto something

that's going to work," she told me. "It's Dr. Cooper's Fabulous Fructose Diet, no calorie counting and no hunger."

"Another eat-as-much-as-you-like diet. What foods this time?"

"No, no. This diet is based on the fact that many people have hypoglycemia, and that's why they can't lose weight. You see, they have low blood sugar, and their hunger alarm is constantly going off. Then they eat something sweet, and the glucose triggers the body's insulin. Insulin should lower the body's glucose, but with a lot of over-weight people like me, too much insulin is sent out by our glands."

I looked at her, bewildered as she went on. "What happens is that the insulin causes the blood sugar to drop too low, and we get hungry again and overeat. The insulin also stimulates fat production in our bodies."

"Well, you certainly seem to know your physiology," I said admiringly. "How do you prevent low blood sugar?"

"By eating fructose. It's a sugar, but sweeter than sucrose (ordinary granulated sugar), and the body burns it up very slowly. On this diet, you eat about thirty grams of fructose daily and stay on a low-calorie diet just as you suggested." She then read a passage from the book to me. "According to *Dr. Cooper's Fabulous Fructose Diet,* which presents a 'calorie deficient diet' plus fructose," she said, "fructose is merely the raw material that will take the stress away from dieting and eliminate hunger."

I could have anticipated Evelyn's experience with the fructose diet. In the beginning some weight came off, but Evelyn is not one to stick with any diet. Eventually she gave it up and started looking for something else. I wasn't surprised when she came back with the Pritikin diet. It didn't seem the kind of program that Evelyn would go into, but now I detected a touch of desperation in her approach.

Once she explained the Pritikin diet to me, I was not at all sure that she would make the grade. The Pritikin program advises two kinds of whole grain daily, raw and cooked vegetables, fruit, beans, peas, sweet potatoes and squash and some, not much, lean animal protein. It also adds unflaked bran for bulk (remember Evelyn's trouble with the low-bulk diet) and three full meals a day. The diet restricts salt, alcohol and coffee. According to Dr. Pritikin, in *The Pritikin Program for Diet and Exercise*, "the Pritikin diet is low in fats, cholesterol, protein and highly refined carbohydrates such as sugar. It is high in starches as part of complex, mostly unrefined carbohydrates."

When I discussed the Pritikin diet with Dr. Gelfand, she nodded. "It's a low-protein, high-carbohydrate diet, but it's based on complex carbohydrates—grains, whole wheat, bread and vegetables. Trouble is, it's a hard diet to stick to because it's unfamiliar to most of us. I particularly like that part about fiber. You know, there may be a close connection between a lack of fiber and cancer, gallstones, varicose veins and even hemorrhoids. However, you can take fiber through what your friend calls the yo-yo effect. If this diet, or any other diet, is: Will it keep the weight off? I see so many of my patients go through what your friend calls the yo-yo effect. If I can make a prediction, Evelyn will take off some weight with this diet and fail to keep it off. She'll be right back to square one, and I can't help thinking all that up and down again with weight isn't doing her body any good, or her heart."

"Well, Evelyn said she was a diet bum and maybe she's right!"


## The Scarsdale Diet

I never did find out what happened to Evelyn, because she quit the gym that month and our paths drifted apart. But I was startled to hear Marie, a friend of my wife, mention the Pritikin diet at dinner one evening. We had laid out a pretty fancy spread, my wife's specialty of *vitello tonnato* and my own famous pomegranate ices. Marie looked at the table with glittering eyes and said, "Thank god I'm off the Pritikin diet!"

"What diet *are* you on?" one of the women asked, unnecessarily I thought, for Marie is nicely rounded and shouldn't lose a speck of it.

"Must everyone be on a diet? Always?" Marie's husband exploded. "All of you look great, for Chrissakes. Why diet?"

"You don't understand, dear," she said, patting his hand. "It so happens I'm not dieting at all right now, tonight." She helped herself to some veal and spooned some tuna sauce over it. "But next week I start the Scarsdale Diet."

"Ah!" A sigh went around the table, and everyone bent to the *vitello tonnato*.

After the guests had left and we were doing up the dishes, I asked my wife what she knew about the Scarsdale Diet.

"Good lord, where have you been? Everyone's

heard of the Scarsdale Diet."

"Does it work?"

She thought about that for a moment. "You know—it seems to. I have a few friends who've tried it. Do you want to go on it?"

I patted my stomach thoughtfully. "First let me read a bit about it."

It was another variation of a high-protein diet. There was a lot about a balanced meal, but the diet itself as pointed out in *The Complete Scarsdale Medical Diet,* "averages 43 percent protein, 22.5 percent fat and 34.5 percent carbohydrate." According to generally accepted nutritional standards, this percentage ratio is unbalanced. It contains about three times as much protein each day as the body needs, half as much fat and a reduced intake of carbohydrates.

Breakfast was the same each day: fruit, protein bread and coffee or tea without cream or sugar. Lunch varied—either fruit salad, canned fish, cold-cuts, eggs or cheese; and dinner had a serving of protein (either lean meat, fish or fowl) and salad. There were some other additions, but no oil or fat.

The big advantage, as I saw it, of the Scarsdale Diet, was its rigidity. It told you exactly what to eat. Substitutions were few and you were advised to stay on it only two weeks. So we decided to try it.

My wife lasted a little short of two weeks. "It's that funny taste in my mouth," she complained. "It's awful."

"It must be the ketones. That happens on any high-protein diet." I remembered what Dr. Gelfand had said about the body's electrolyte balance, and I shook my head. "We'd better quit now, while we're ahead."

"Or behind," she corrected me admiring herself in the mirror. "I did lose five pounds."

I had lost weight, too, but in the next few weeks the lost weight seemed to drift back on. "Isn't there any diet," my wife complained, "that we could go on without all the fuss and bother; a diet that would take the weight off and keep it off?"

"That's another chapter," I told her, making my plans then and there.

# 6

# *TAKE IT OFF, TAKE IT OFF!*

### *The Human Machine*

Now pay attention, gentle readers, I'm about to let you in on the final, the ultimate, the all-time truth about dieting. Once you read and understand and absorb this bit of ancient wisdom and put it into practice, losing weight will be guaranteed, safe and absolutely certain!

Does that sound like wild exaggeration? Personally, I hate to indulge in this type of extravagant promise because it's a direct invitation for the writer to end up with egg on his face. A goodly percentage of my readers are going to flub this weight-loss business for one reason or another. That's why I tend to qualify everything I write about dieting. (An unkind editor once called it weasel-wording.) But the truth is, instead of hard-to-keep promises, it's easier to say, *In some cases . . .* or *It may . . .* or *Possibly . . . It often happens . . .* and so on. Nevertheless, the "tremendous secret" I'm about to disclose is based on a law of physics that has to do with the conservation of energy. Physicists usually don't weasel-word. They come right out and state their laws dogmatically, and I'll do the same—or try to.

The law: *Your weight is a function of the food you take in and the energy you expend.* Simple? Well, that's it. To lose weight in a healthy fashion, forget about high-protein diets, or high-fat diets, or high-carbohydrate diets or any exotic combination of the three. Concentrate only on one simple fact of nature. The human body is a machine that runs on the energy provided by food.

Now an automobile is a machine that runs on the energy provided by gasoline. How far it will go depends on how much gas you put into it. Some autos are more efficient than others and will go farther. The auto converts gas to energy and uses that energy to move ahead.

The human machine converts food to energy and uses that energy to move, to think, to live. Oh, we are built a bit more cleverly than an auto. For example: If an auto is given too much gasoline, it just spills the extra out of the tank. If a human is given too much food, that extra food is stored as fat inside the body. When the human machine has no outside fuel available, it uses up its stored fat.

The automobile may take five gallons of gas to go a hundred miles if it's an efficient subcompact model. The human body uses up X calories to power it through a normal day. As long as we eat enough food to supply us with X calories, we neither lose our stored fat nor store any more. We do not lose weight, nor do we gain.

But increase our food from X to X + 1 and we will store that one calorie as fat, or decrease the fuel to X-1 and we will use up one calorie of stored fat.

"That may be so," my fat friend George complains, "but even if our bodies act like that, we are not machines. We are human and each different from the other. I eat exactly what my friend Tom eats. I put on the pounds and Tom doesn't change. He's like a rail. He eats like a horse and he's still too thin to throw a shadow!"

This may or may not be true. The chances are

that George still out-eats Tom. But to get back to the auto simile, and run it into the ground a bit, I'm sure each of us has at one time or another owned one of those maddening gas guzzlers that gets about eight miles to the gallon. We can never understand why our neighbor with the same model car gets ten to fifteen miles. Something has to be wrong with our machine. In the same way, something is wrong with Tom's skinny body. He doesn't utilize his calories as well as George does. His body is inefficient, while George's body is superefficient.

But efficient or not, the same law of the conservation of energy holds. Starve both George and Tom, and they'll both lose weight. Tom needs his X amount of calories to function. Cut them in half and he'll waste away. If his inefficient body has never stored fat, he will use his own muscles as fuel. Cut George's X supply of calories in half, and he too will lose weight. But he'll lose his stored fat.

Although to George, Tom seems the desirable way to be, the truth is that George functions more efficiently. What he has not learned in all the years of his life is his own exact X requirement of calories. Those of us who are overweight like George have not, for one reason or another, come to grips with the fact that we are eating more food than we need to fuel our bodies. Actually George is no better off than Tom. Just more efficient. His fat does him no good.

## Clyde's Belly

Clyde, a forty-year-old neighbor of mine in the country, works as a contractor. He's a muscular man, tall and good-looking, but with a large paunch. "My beer belly," he calls it laughing, but with a hurt, bewildered look way back in his eyes.

Once Clyde showed me a snapshot of himself taken when he was twenty-three. It was at the beach and he's laughing into the camera. His face looks the way it is now, with a bit more hair and a few less wrinkles, but his body! Slim and well-muscled, the same broad shoulders, but a tapered waist and flat stomach—a lean, trim young man.

With a sigh, Clyde put the picture away. "I can't understand it. Where the hell did all my fat come from?"

"From what you eat," I suggested.

"Hey, come on! I eat exactly what I ate then. Okay, so I like my beer, but I drank as much when I was a kid, and I ate the same meals. No, I figure it's my glands. I made an appointment with my doctor. I want him to try some thyroid on me. Maybe that'll help."

I tried to talk Clyde out of taking thyroid. It's a common, last-ditch effort for many fat people. The thyroid gland controls the body's metabolism —how we burn up our food. It can be compared to a carburetor on a car. Sometimes our "carburetor" goes wrong, and weight is put on too quickly, while the body slows down and becomes lethargic. Sometimes when the thyroid puts out too much hormone, the body is speeded up, and too much fuel is consumed. But most cases of over-weight have nothing to do with the thyroid. Too much fat affects every part of our bodies including our thyroid glands, but then it's the fat, not the thyroid that's to blame.

Clyde's real problem was very simple and very common. The majority of overweight people in America suffer from it. During their early years

92

they are very physical, very active. They burn up their food efficiently, and they get into the habit of eating enough to cover their energy expenditure. Very active people—athletes, hard working laborers, housewives—burn up a lot of food and can eat a great deal without storing any. Clyde was like that. He worked hard as a laborer in construction and was proud of his physical ability; and he ate accordingly.

Trouble was, as he became more successful, he began to do less physical work, and eventually he became a successful contractor, married, had children and cut his physical activity way down. What stayed the same was the amount of food he ate and the amount of beer he drank. Because it was an efficient machine, his body began to store all that extra food as fat—potential fuel for the lean times to come. Unfortunately for Clyde, those lean times never came.

When I met him after his doctor's visit, he seemed very depressed. "What's wrong?" I asked.

"That damned doctor says he won't try thyroid! My BMR, whatever the hell that is, is normal. I don't know; I guess I'll have to live with it."

"Your BMR is your basal metabolic rate, the rate at which your body burns up your food. Hell, if it's normal, you should be glad."

"Glad? When I've got this encumbrance?" He slapped his belly.

"Clyde," I said thoughtfully, "I'll make you a deal. Be a guinea pig for me and I'll get rid of that belly for you."

"What kind of a guinea pig?"

"I want you to try out a new diet."

Uneasily, he said, "I just can't diet. I get weak and headachy and irritable."

"Not on this one. Anyway, you've got a simple choice. Your belly or my diet. Which is it going to be?"

Clyde considered, chewing his lip. Finally he nodded. "Okay, you've got your pig."

And that's how the first man to test my diet agreed.


## Fataway

I've fallen into the acronym trap, and I've decided my new diet should be called the FATAWAY diet. It stands for *Fast's Absolutely Terrific And Warranted, Assured, Youthful* diet. Before I share it with you, there are some principles that must be understood. One is a corollary of the law of the conservation of energy. "You spend or store what you take in." And this raises the question, "How much should I take in?" This, in turn, depends on how much energy you spend in a day. And of course, we are talking about energy in terms of calories.

We can get some help here from the Food and Nutrition Board of the National Academy of Science. They have published a table of the recommended energy intake, which (if you are neither to lose nor gain) should be equal to our energy output. Here is an adaptation of the table.

| Age of Men | Range of Calories Expended in an Average Day* |
|---|---|
| 19 years to 22 | 2,500 to 3,300 |
| 23 years to 50 | 2,300 to 3,100 |
| 51 years to 75 | 2,000 to 2,800 |
| Over 75 years | 1,650 to 2,450 |

| Age of Women | Range of Calories Expended in an Average Day* |
|---|---|
| 19 years to 22 | 1,700 to 2,500 |
| 23 years to 50 | 1,600 to 2,400 |
| 51 years to 75 | 1,400 to 2,200 |
| Over 75 years | 1,200 to 2,000 |

\* Of course, the energy expended will vary according to height and weight as well as activity. These figures are for moderately active people at a desirable weight of 154 pounds for men who are five feet ten inches tall, and for women who are 120 pounds of weight with a height of five feet, three inches. Most variations in weight and height will still fall close to this average expenditure of calories.

We can see from this table that as we grow older, our necessary caloric intake—the amount of fuel we need to run our human machines—decreases. If like Clyde you keep stoking your machine with the same amount of food you ate when you were young, the excess will be stored as fat. Look around at all your friends and neighbors over forty, and you'll see that storage at work.

Let us say my typical dieter is forty years old—a man like Clyde, for example. How much food does he need a day to maintain equilibrium? To neither gain nor lose?

For Clyde, that would be about 2,700 calories. If we put Clyde on a 2,000 calories a day diet, he would begin to lose weight, but it might be a long time before it showed. If it took too long, he could easily become discouraged. Clyde would do well on a 1,600 calorie a day diet or even a 1,200 calorie diet. He'd begin to see his weight loss after a week, and he'd feel encouraged enough to stick to the diet. As an added bonus, the chances are he wouldn't be too hungry on this diet.

Most men under seventy-five years of age would lose weight comfortably on a 1,600 calorie diet, and so would women who are large. (The larger you are the more fuel you need to operate. Think of a truck and a compact in terms of gas use.) For most women and some smaller men, a diet of 1,200 calories a day would do nicely to lose weight. It would be a comfortable, gradual process, but fast enough to be encouraging. There is no reason, however, why anyone should not try the 1,200-calorie-a-day diet to start.

### Balancing It All

A low-calorie diet is the first step to losing weight, but the second step, and a very important one, is a nutritionally balanced diet. I fully believe it's better to remain slightly overweight and eat a proper diet than to lose weight on a high-protein, high-carbohydrate or high-fat diet. The balanced diet keeps you healthy and keeps you from getting too hungry. It also reeducates you in terms of eating. One certainty, you'll never go hungry on the FATAWAY diet.

Beverly Daniel, my friendly nutritionist, suggested to me that whenever you diet you should check with your doctor to see if you need a multivitamin and mineral capsule each day. "You should, of course, try to get all your nutritional elements from your diet," she said, "but just to play it safe, you could take the vitamins and minerals. There's no need for any megavitamin doses; in fact, they may be very dangerous. I, myself, would never, never take megavitamins without a doctor's recommendation."

"Which type of vitamins are best," I asked her, "natural or snythetic?"

"The cheapest you can buy. They're all government controlled, and that whole nonsensical bit about natural vitamins doesn't make sense. Get a cheap, complete vitamin capsule. That's all."

A nutritionally balanced diet, Beverly drummed into me, should be made up of:

| | |
|---|---|
| 50 percent carbohydrates... | These should include whole grains, vegetables and fruits. |
| 30 percent fat..... | For health reasons stick to poly-unsaturated fats. |
| 20 percent protein......... | Remember that even lean meat has some fat in it. Although the diet doesn't seem to include much fat, your protein source will add fat to it. Fish is excellent on a diet and poultry is a good source of protein, especially without the skin. |
| | However, these percentages do not have to be rigid. You can always cut down on the fats safely. It will help weight loss. |

Both Beverly and Dr. Gelfand advised cutting down on sodium, especially for older dieters—older starting at forty. Beverly pointed out that MSG (monosodium glutamate, a very ubiquitous flavoring agent in commercially prepared foods) actually yields more sodium than table salt.

"Watch out for it in bouillon cubes which can have salt too. Check the labels."

One final word before I present the FATAWAY diet. You must, if you wish to lose weight, stick to this diet with *fanatical devotion*. The only options you have are those I specifically give you. The rules of the game are very rigid. Break just one and the FATAWAY will fail. Stick to it all, and you've got it made!

## The Rules of the Game

1. Make sure you are in good health, aside from being fat. I would suggest checking out the diet with your doctor first.

2. You may drink as much water as you wish.

3. You may drink tea or coffee, provided you use no cream, just milk in the coffee, and no sugar. You can use artificial sweeteners. Now the caffeine in both tea and coffee is of doubtful value and may be harmful to your health. More and more studies seem to implicate it in a number of conditions. Women with cystic breast disease, for example, have had good results when they cut out tea and coffee (and chocolate and coke, two other sources of caffeine). I've found that a good substitute drink can be made out of chicory once you get used to the rather sweet taste. Brew it just as you would coffee. Herb teas too, if they have no caffeine, are good.

4. You can add soup to any meal if you make it out of bouillon cubes (without salt) or skim the fat off cooked broth. Salad dressing can be made with a yogurt base, adding lemon juice or vinegar or

tomato juice, or any combination of these with spices, pepper, paprika, garlic, mustard—you'll find you can blend a very tasty salad dressing without oils.

5. These are the *NO-NO's*. You *must* avoid all of the following:

*Alcoholic beverages of any sort:* Beer, wine, liquor. (You can cook with wine because boiling gets rid of the alcohol.)

*The following fruits and vegetables:* Avocados, dried fruits, dried peas or beans, lima beans, lentils, coconut, potatoes, olives, rice, soybeans.

*These meat and dairy products:* Cold-cuts, bacon, butter, sweet and sour cream.

*These baked products:* Cake, cookies, crackers, doughnuts, pretzels, pies, pancakes, waffles.

*Sweets:* Candy, chocolate, honey, ice cream, ices and sherbets, jams, jellies, puddings, sugar, syrup.

*Pastas:* Spaghetti, macaroni, noodles and all other pasta!

*And:* All salad dressings that are not made by you according to instructions, gravy, margarine, mayonnaise, nuts, peanut butter, popcorn, sodas.

6. These are the *YES-YES's*, what you *can* eat.

You should have two eight-ounce glasses of skim milk or buttermilk each day, at meals or in between, or as a bedtime snack. You can substitute eight ounces of fat-free yogurt for one glass of milk. The yogurt is valuable in cooking.

You can eat as much as you want of the following vegetables, either raw or cooked. If cooked, they should be prepared without oil or fat.

They can serve as snacks between meals, or whenever you feel a bout of the "famishes" coming on, or as "crudities" at any meal:

asparagus
broccoli
cabbage
cauliflower
celery
cucumber
endive
escarole
lettuce
bean sprouts
mushrooms
peppers
pickles (as long as they're not sweet)
radishes
sauerkraut
spinach
watercress

7. Each day you *must* have at least one portion of any one of the following vegetables, but you *can* have two portions:

artichokes
beets
brussels sprouts
carrots
eggplant
kohlrabi
string beans
tomatoes
onions
parsnips
peas
pumpkin
scallions

winter squash
turnips

## How to Cook Your Food on the FATAWAY Diet

Bake, broil, roast or poach all your meat, fish and poultry. Trim off all the fat you can. To avoid drying these foods out while broiling them, use thicker cuts, baste with salt-free bouillon or mustard or yogurt mixed with tomato juice and flavored with your favorite spice. Baste fish with lemon juice or poach in tomato juice and water, again properly spiced.

Eggs should either be poached in water with a spoonful of vinegar to hold the yolk together, or boiled in the shell, or scrambled in a stick-free pan.

Vegetables may be eaten raw or cooked with lemon juice, vinegar, salt-free bouillon, tomato juice, plain water or steamed.

Fruit should be eaten raw or cooked without sugar. If you must use canned fruit, prepare it about an hour before you eat by washing it with hot water to get rid of the sugar syrup and then chilling it.

## And now the FATAWAY Diet

As I explained, there are two diet plans. One gives you 1,200 calories a day and is suitable for the average woman and small man. The other gives 1,600 calories a day and works well for average men and large women. The two diet plans are exactly the same, except that the 1,600 calorie diet uses *half a pound* portions of meat, poultry or fish for dinner instead of *a quarter pound* as the 1,200 calorie diet does. Beverly Daniel suggests starting with the 1,200 calorie diet. "Some people just don't lose weight fast enough on the 1,600 calorie diet."

## BREAKFASTS

All breakfasts are the same each morning, although there is room for individual variation.

- One orange, or one-half grapefruit, or four ounces of orange juice or eight ounces of tomato juice. (The tomato juice can be divided into four ounces at breakfast and the other four ounces at dinner.)
- One egg, poached, boiled or scrambled in a stick-free pan, but only three eggs a week. You can substitute two tablespoons of cottage cheese for eggs.
- One slice of whole-grain bread, plain or toasted.
- Coffee, tea, or any similar beverage. Whole milk can be used in the coffee, but no sugar. Artificial sweeteners such as saccharin can be used.

## LUNCHES

*Monday:* Cottage cheese salad. This is made with four ounces of cottage cheese and raw vegetables or fruit cut in. Any amount of raw vegetables can be used, but fruit, if used, should be limited to two pieces. Lettuce can also be added. One slice of whole-grain bread and a beverage: tea, coffee, skimmed milk or any diet soda.

*Tuesday:* Open-faced, melted cheese sandwich. This is made from two ounces of any hard cheese. Bean sprouts and mustard or any preferred spice can be placed on two slices of bread. The grated cheese is then sprinkled over this and the sandwiches are grilled till the cheese is melted. This is served with "crudities," (any selection of raw vegetables) and the usual beverages.

*Wednesday:* Tuna salad. Three ounces of canned tuna, water-packed, is used for the salad (canned salmon can be substituted). Chop up cucumber, celery, radishes and some watercress and add to crumbled tuna. For dressing, use a low fat yogurt base flavored with your own choice of spices. Serve on a bed of lettuce with one slice of whole-grain bread and your choice of beverages.

*Thursday:* Hamburger. Use three ounces of lean hamburger (it's preferable to trim and chop the meat yourself if possible). Shape into a patty and broil. Serve with mustard and pickles on two slices of whole-grain bread. Sliced onion and tomato and lettuce are good with this, or a small tossed green salad with your own dressing. Finish off with choice of beverage.

*Friday:* Four ounces of cottage cheese in a salad or plain with vegetables. (This can be varied from Monday's lunch by making one with fruit and the other with vegetables.) Serve on a bed of lettuce with sliced cucumbers and tomatoes, and with one slice of bread.

*Saturday:* Cold poached fish. Use either salmon, striped bass, or any fish that takes well to poaching. One good method is to layer carrots, celery, onions and garlic, all sliced, on the bottom of the pan. Add your favorite spices, and pour in enough liquid to half-cover the fish. (Wine can be used here, since the alcohol boils away during the cooking.) Let it come to a boil, and then either cook slowly on top of the stove until it's done or bake in a 350-degree oven. In both methods you baste during the cooking. This fish is delicious served hot, but can also be served cold with a sauce made of watercress cooked for ten minutes and cucumber mixed in a blender with yogurt and your favorite spices. Serve with one slice of whole-grain bread, a tossed salad and your choice of beverage.

*Sunday:* Chicken. Three ounces. This is a bit tricky since the bones don't count in weighing your portion. A good trick is to take the meat from a boiled chicken, and mix three ounces of it into a curry sauce made of yogurt, curry and other spices. A bouillon cube dissolved in a tablespoon of hot water makes a good starting base for the sauce. Add the yogurt, then the curry, some thyme, diced onions and green pepper and you've got a fine low-calorie curry sauce. Add the chicken meat and heat. Serve with any two cooked vegetables and some crudities, a slice of whole-grain bread and a beverage.


### DINNERS


*Monday:* This is steak night. Use one-quarter of a pound of lean sirloin, cut thick. Broil it with mushrooms and onions. These can be braised with a touch of bouillon. Serve with either carrots or squash and a green vegetable. Try a spinach salad of raw spinach leaves, sliced raw mushrooms and your favorite dressing. One slice of whole-grain bread and your favorite fruit for dessert. Top it off with your favorite low-calorie beverage.

*Tuesday:* Fish tonight. A quarter pound of fresh fish. I would suggest broiling it. Put a filet skin side down on aluminum foil. Spread lemon juice over the top and sprinkle with paprika. Broil about four inches from the flame (to keep it from drying out) and broil for eight to twelve minutes depending on thickness. Serve with two cooked vegetables and a green tossed salad. Fruit, but no bread tonight, (you had two slices at lunch) and a beverage.

*Wednesday:* Chicken. Try a chicken breast, one quarter pound portion, baked with a spoonful of Parmesan cheese, tomato juice and spices. Two cooked vegetables (try for a yellow one) crudities and a slice of whole-grain bread. Dessert is fruit. All this fruit for desserts could be a bore, but you can vary the desserts by poaching pears, for instance, or baking apples using no sugar. Or you could serve washed and chilled canned fruits and a beverage.

*Thursday:* Stuffed fish. Try a filet of sole or flounder wrapped around a filling of chopped spinach and mushrooms bound with a touch of yogurt and (sacrificing half your slice of bread) toasted bread crumbs. Bake the stuffed fillet for fifteen minutes at 350 degrees. Serve with vegetables and a salad. Try tomatoes and chopped fresh basil with a yogurt dressing. Add some crushed cumin seeds and chill for two hours before serving. Bread, fruit and beverage.

*Friday:* One quarter pound of roast lamb with turnips and squash, or if you hate those, try some other vegetables, preferably something that can be roasted with the meat and flavored with its juices. The roast needn't be too lean. Presumably it will last for other meals. One slice of bread, fruit and beverage.

*Saturday:* Let's try a veal stew. Cut up a quarter pound of veal. Stew it in tomato juice spiced up and thickened after cooking with yogurt. Another thickening agent allowed on the diet is okra. Spices are really what will make the difference here. Serve with a spinach and mushroom salad and vegetables. One slice of bread, fruit and a beverage.

*Sunday:* Shrimp. Use the largest you can buy and serve four as a helping. Broil them and serve with a mustard and yogurt sauce, or any other sauce you can devise. You can treat yourself to a tablespoon of butter—after all, it's Sunday night. Mash garlic into the butter and put a touch on each shrimp before broiling. No bread tonight. (Did you think you were getting away with those butter calories?) But you can have your fruit and beverage.


## Confessions

So you have your diet. If you stick with it truthfully, your weight loss will be steady and gradual—for a while. Inevitably, you will reach a plateau. Plateauing is a common occurrence. It's almost as if the body reaches a point of resistance and says, "I just won't lose any more unless you make me!" It's up to you to make it. How? By sticking to the diet during that discouraging period even when it seems to deny the law of conservation of energy. It can last a while, but after the plateau, you'll begin to lose weight again, not as dramatically as in the beginning, but it will come off.

Clyde, my friend with the big belly, tried this diet for me, and it worked very well. He lost weight rapidly at first, then reached the usual plateau. Fortunately, he stuck with the diet and now his gut is a thing of the past. His next step, he tells me, is to get into "shape" again.

Finally, before I end this chapter. I have a confession to make. FATAWAY is not an original diet of my own. I can claim credit only for sprucing it up a bit and putting a few flourishes on it. The material in it is based on nutritional guidelines issued by the United States Department of Agriculture and the United States Department of Health, Education and Welfare. My confession may make me a tad less original as a dietician, but I think it adds a touch of authenticity. It's a diet you can have faith in, and the good part is that it's a diet you can stick to as long as you wish. It's balanced and nutritious and with some ingenuity it can be very satisfying. I've tried to jazz it up a bit, but I'm sure any thoughtful reader can do even more. The best of luck with it.

# 7

## KEEPING IT OFF

### Stacy's Success Story

I talked to my old friend Stacy one afternoon while we were out walking, and I told her how proud of her I was. "You look wonderful. As pretty as the day you were married."

And pretty she was, not only her face, but her figure as well—her new figure, I should say, for Stacy had started dieting five months ago, and so far she had lost forty-three pounds. She had twenty-five more to go, but already the bloated look, the jowls and heavy hips were gone. She still looked overweight, but nothing like her former roly-poly self.

"I've been fat for ten years," she told me. "I began to blow up right after my wedding, and I just kept going."

"Did you ever try to diet before this?" I asked.

"Oh hell, I tried all the diets, the Stillman, the Atkins, and I'd always lose some weight, but then stop and put it all back on. Once I ate nothing but grapefruit and coffee for a solid week. Then back to the sweets and starches."

"Well, this time you seem to be on your way."

"You're right. I took myself in hand and decided this is it, a simple 1,000 calorie diet based on your FATAWAY diet, but cut down here and there. I don't like eggs, and they were easy to do without.''

"One thousand calories! That's pretty low."

"Yeah, but I was pretty fat. Anyway, I wanted some quick results to encourage myself. I have enough stored fat to burn up. Even at 1,000 calories, I keep the diet well-balanced. You've taught me that.''

"After all these years, what made you decide to finally do it?''

She was thoughtful as we walked along, and after a while she said, ''Before my mother died, she told me that the one thing that would make her happy was my taking off weight—and I couldn't do it. And now, three years later, just like that, I told my husband we're going on a diet. He was about thirty pounds overweight, and I think it was my concern for his health that did it. We were both too fat, but his high blood pressure was going up and that scared me. Maybe it was that, and maybe because nobody was pressuring me. I used to feel such terrible guilt at the way Mom felt about my weight. That's gone now. My husband and I went on the diet at once, no if's and's or but's, and we've stuck to it. I'll tell you something else. Once all my excess weight is off, it won't come back. I just know it.''

Stacy said she felt better now than she ever had —more confident, more assured, but was that one of the reasons why she was able to lose the weight, or was that a result of the weight loss? ''I think it works both ways,'' she told me thoughtfully.

Taking off weight is hard enough. Keeping it off is much harder. It's not easy to stop the yo-yo effect, but in the months that followed Stacy managed it. She reached the weight she wanted, and stayed right there. One of the things that happened, she confessed, was her re-education in terms of food. "I took a lot of weight off at first, then, a while after I talked to you, I plateaued. Almost a month went by with no weight loss while I stuck to that 1,000-calorie-a-day diet. That was really rough. Every morning I'd get on the scales, and it was bad news! I wasn't losing an ounce. I stayed right there at 148 pounds for a solid month! If I were going to break, that's when it would have happened.

"My husband told me, 'If you're going to be a pessimist, you'll say I haven't lost an ounce on the diet, but if you're an optimist, you'll say, Hey, I haven't gained an ounce!'

"Then, very slowly, not as dramatically as at first, the weight began to come off again. But the interesting point is, when I was down to the weight I wanted to reach, I didn't go off the diet. I simply expanded it."

"In what way?"

"I kept our meals balanced, following the mix of fat, protein and carbohydrate you suggested in your FATAWAY diet. I didn't add any cake or candy or ice cream. We put more oil into salad dressings, maybe have a bit of pasta now and then. Once a week I have a frozen yogurt pop at 160 calories, but then I've done that all through the diet. It satisfies my craving for sweets—although I must say my craving has lessened. But now my husband and I eat within the framework of a nutritionally sound diet. Dinner is meat, fish or poultry, vegetables and a salad. We've kicked the dessert habit, except sometimes we have berries, melon or some other fruit. Lunch for me is cheese, fruit and crackers. My husband eats lunch out at work, but he keeps it simple. Anyway, he burns up more calories than I do. Our breakfast? It's always the same, juice and toast, whole-grained cereal or egg. Oh, sometimes we eat bread for lunch, but rarely sandwiches. If we go out, we eat normally, but don't overdo it. Our entire eating pattern has changed. We're perfectly happy with it, and I think the weight is off to stay."

## The Anonymous Overeater

Unfortunately, not all dieters are as successful as Stacy. In the course of preparing this book I ran into a group who feel that taking the weight off was the smallest part of the problem. Keeping it off was everything. Marty, a social worker, first talked to me about this group. You wouldn't think Marty had a weight problem. If he was overweight at all, it was surely no more than ten pounds, and yet he considered himself a compulsive eater.

"The only way I've kept my weight down and my life normal," he said, to my surprise, "is by joining Overeaters Anonymous."

When I asked about the organization, he suggested that I go to one of the meetings, and I took down the address of the nearest one.

There were over thirty people who showed up for the session in one of the meeting rooms at New York's Memorial Hospital. The age range was twenty to sixty, and the majority were women. In fact, including myself, there were only six men. Some of us sat on either side of a long table, and the rest in chairs against the wall, and it seemed to me that there was a general air of quiet desperation, and as the meeting went on, a forced friendliness.

Only a few of the group could qualify as obese. Some were overweight, but most seemed normal and a few were quite thin. The meeting started with everyone holding hands and repeating a *serenity prayer*. We all took turns reading from a list of 12 rules or precepts, and I felt a strong undertone of religion, as if they all were counting on a higher power, religion or God, for help in controlling their overeating.

A young woman spoke up and told us the last month had been terrible for her. Her brother and uncle had died and her mother had been in a car accident. She had reacted by overeating, but now she felt that sharing her troubles with the group took the pressure off her. Anton, a young doctor who led the meeting, had come down in weight from 240 pounds to 160 without consciously dieting. He had lost the weight once he understood why he overate, but he could only do this if he was in touch with a higher power. He still felt fat. "Former fat people," he insisted, "always have a fat mentality."

Anton understood himself better after hearing other people talk about their problem. "Today I live my life without concern about food," he concluded. "I used to eat all the time. I had an insane need for food. I would sometimes go out at midnight, desperately searching for some all-night grocery or deli."

"My name is Sally," an attractive, slim young woman announced, and I winced as the group chorused, "Hello, Sally!" in perfect unison. A deep, inner privacy kept me from this immediate, and to me forced, conviviality. But it seemed to work for the group. I could see that it enabled Sally to talk more easily. She was a compulsive over-eater. "I have to speak up, though I hate to. I have trouble accepting the fact that I have a disease. Yes, I honestly feel overeating is a disease, but still I keep stuffing myself. There has to be something wrong with me." Her voice became intense, fearful. "I get so scared. When I begin to eat compulsively, everything is covered with a gathering blackness." She stopped abruptly, sagging with exhaustion mixed with a curious sense of relief.

Eileen spoke up. "I'm a compulsive overeater. I don't want to feel full of food, and I don't know why I do it. My sponsor says I should call her, but how can I call her at three or four in the morning? I don't know why I gorge. I want good things for myself, but why do I do this to me?"

The sponsor concept is an important part of Overeaters Anonymous (OA). Everyone is supposed to have a sponsor, a more experienced member of OA, who can be called at any time to help with advice, to share experiences or just to be there as a sounding board.

Graham, an intense dark-eyed man in his thirties, spoke up. He was disturbed by the meeting, and he had prayed, asking the Lord what he could do. "The Lord told me to say something that frightens me," Graham told us. "I have to speak of that blackness of Sally's. I've come to understand that I know nothing about myself, my desires, where I'm going, how I'm getting there. The only way I can survive is through my connection with God. I feel the dark force is Satan, it's a battle between God and Satan, and you must hold onto God. Abstinence from food comes by praying for it, asking God for it every day. I've stayed abstinent four months now, and I hope to stay that way the rest of my life!''

There was an awkward silence after Graham's deeply religious speech. Abstinence, in OA terminology, means refraining from all eating between planned meals and all "binge" foods.

Sarah, middle-aged and tightly corseted, said, "I used to think I only binged when I felt bad, but now I see that I binge even when I feel good. I don't understand it!''

Binging, or pigging out on one particular type of food, seems to be a problem with compulsive over-eaters. They will stay on a diet until temptation in the form of a dish of ice cream, a handful of peanuts or a slice of cake gets the better of them, and then, wham! A half gallon of ice cream, a whole can of peanuts, an entire cake—and that's only the beginning. They seem to become wild, un-controllable, ravenous for food. In a startling way, it seemed like the other side of the coin of the problem faced by many of the anorexic young women I had interviewed.

One woman told us she felt the need to eat only when something terrible happened, when she was lonely or unhappy. Another said she didn't under-stand why she was driven to binge when all went well. "I'm a natural born self-destructor, and my job in life seems to be to screw myself up. Whatever happens, I want to get into food, like a pig into garbage.''

The meeting went on with the same theme repeated again and again. By overeating, they felt they were doing something wicked to themselves. It was a form of self-degradation. Most had no knowledge of why they binged, but felt they could control this destructive urge only by throwing themselves on God's mercy. They needed a "higher power." Others could only resist food if they took life one day at a time.

As a group, it seemed to me that they had completely lost touch with themselves. They had to look somewhere else, to other members of the group or to their "higher power" for love, strength and support.

The least important part of the program, I realized, was the diet. The most important part was the list of 12 steps in which members admit they are powerless and promise to trust themselves to a higher authority, a strength greater than themselves. To most of them this was God. To some, it was the group itself.

A psychiatrist who specializes in weight loss and who has worked with OA, feels the group causes a shift in the members' emotional states, "a move away from negative feeling to positive ones, something like a spiritual conversion." There may be slip-ups, he maintained, but as long as compulsive overeaters attend the group, they can get help. Associating with other compulsive overeaters gives them hope. They aren't judged, ridiculed or scolded. Just supported.

Does Overeaters Anonymous work? I don't know of any scientific study that has followed them for any length of time, but they claim to have 100,000 members worldwide, and that tells us something.

In my experience, I found that most of the members I met were not tremendously overweight, although they all told me that at one time they had been. One long-time member told me that compulsive eaters, such as members of OA, use food as a drug when they are unhappy, depressed, angry, disappointed, neglected or sad, or oddly enough, even when they're happy. It's a way of covering up emotions that are too strong to handle. Food acts as an anesthetic agent, a pacifier. In that sense compulsive eating is an addiction.

The fact that many OAs regard their compulsive eating as a disease that cannot be cured is very much like Alcoholics Anonymous' approach to drinking. OA itself, in fact, is associated with AA and uses much of its literature. If overeating, like alcoholism, *is* an addiction, there is no simple cure to the problem. The compulsive eater, even when he has licked the habit, is at risk, like the alcoholic, for the rest of his life.

Then the serious problem is, how do you know if you are a compulsive overeater? One positive test was suggested by OA. Read the following questions and answer each honestly by checking the box that applies:

| | Yes | No |
|---|---|---|
| 1. Do you eat when you're not hungry? | | |
| 2. Do you go on eating binges for no reason? | | |
| 3. Do you feel guilty and remorseful after eating? | | |
| 4. Do you give a great deal of time and thought to food? | | |
| 5. Do you look forward eagerly to eating alone? | | |
| 6. Do you plan secret binges ahead of time? | | |
| 7. Do you eat sensibly in front of others, but pig out when you're alone? | | |
| 8. Is your weight affecting the way you live? | | |
| 9. Have you tried and failed at dieting? | | |
| 10. Do you resent others telling you to use | | |

116

11. **Although it isn't so, do you still keep insisting you can diet on your own whenever you wish?**

12. **Do you crave food outside of mealtimes?**

13. **Do you turn to food when you're troubled or worried?**

14. **Does your overeating make you or others unhappy?**

If you answered *yes* to three or more questions, you're in trouble, and you either have an overeating problem or you are on your way to having one. What can you do about it? Well, you can try OA. They have meetings all over the country, or if you aren't gregarious but still want to try their principles on your own, here are a few suggestions:

● Never allow yourself any self-pity because you can't take a snack the way normal people do without going hog-wild over the food.

● Don't permit yourself to think or talk about any real or imagined pleasure you get from certain foods.

● Don't ever believe a bite or two will make a bad situation better. It will only make it worse.

● Think how great it will be, once you're rid of this compulsion, to be free also of guilt and self-hatred, to be free of fearing what other people think about you, free of their pity and contempt—and free of fearing yourself!

## Modifying the Way We Behave

Weight Watchers, another program for the compulsive overeater, does not have the religious overlay that OA has, nor the intensity and fervor. It lacks the anonymous quality of OA, and it puts the blame squarely on the erring eater. You must account for your sins instead of turning to the group for comfort in your sinful state.

But one overweight friend of mine told me she had left Weight Watchers because she couldn't take the constant sense of failure she felt the group inspired in her. "I had to weigh in every time, and if I hadn't lost any weight, or if I had, God forbid, gained some, I felt guilty and self-conscious."

Aside from the approach of constant weighing and checking, which in fact works for some people, Weight Watchers does supply group support and a good nutritious diet. The one flaw from where the dieter stands is the need for continuing help and continuing expenses, for unlike OA, Weight Watchers is not free. This requires ongoing commitment to the program. It works best when you stay in it and are continuously vigilant about your weight.

If religion is not your bag, and a group form of monitoring turns you off, what is the answer to re-shaping your shape? According to a newsletter from Harvard Medical School, the only good cure for obesity is permanently to substitute good eating and drinking habits for poor ones. Fad diets, the health letter says, make their inventors rich, but they do not lead to stable weight loss because they do not modify eating behavior.

To modify our behavior in regard to food seems to be the answer, and here psychology has stepped in with its behavior modification theories. John B. Watson first explored this aspect of psychology back in 1912, and in 1938 B. F. Skinner, opposing Pavlov's theories about conditioned reflexes, suggested that people behave to get a reward.

In 1967 Dr. Albert Stunkard, Chairman of the University of Pennsylvania's Department of Psychology, gave us some good news and some bad news about obesity. First the bad news. According to Dr. Stunkard, of the people who get treatment for obesity, "most will not lose weight. Of those who do lose weight, most will regain it." That's bad, but now for some good news. "Behavior therapy is one of the more promising exceptions!"

Dr. Stunkard believes that the treatment of obesity with behavior modification is the most significant advance in years. Dr. Stunkard's method has four steps.

The first: Eliminate the reinforcements that support your overeating.

The second: Have enough motivation to change your behavior.

The third: Have enough incentive to change.

The fourth: Be realistic about your goals.

The rationale behind Dr. Stunkard's program is that before you can learn how to eat properly, you must notice, analyze and understand the way you *do* eat. He suggests a number of devices, some as simple as putting down your fork between bites to slow your rate of eating. Others include keeping careful records of food eaten, how you felt when you ate, what was happening in your life at that time, your physical activity and other factors.

Self-monitoring is what Dr. Stunkard calls this

process, and he says it can lead to changes in your own behavior. He suggests keeping two books, a Diet Diary and a Daily Log. You make a notation in the diary every time you eat, putting down how much you eat, its caloric content, the time, place, people present and just how you felt. This diary, when you look back at it, should show you which situations prompted you to overeat.

The Daily Log is a list of all the little tricks suggested by the behavior modification program and how well you stuck to them. The self-monitoring involved in keeping both these records is most effective when you make your notations right after you eat or just before.

An important part of the behavior modification program is to limit your contact with food and with the situations that make you eat too much. Some of the program's suggestions bear repeating. Here's a list that may help you to change your eating habits:

- Make low calorie snacks available. For example, keep celery and carrot sticks in a glass in the refrigerator so they confront you when you open it.
- Don't eat while watching television or reading.
- Eat only in one place, the kitchen or the dining room.
- Always leave some food on your plate.
- Leave the table at once when you finish.
- Use tricks to slow your rate of eating, such as putting down your fork between each mouthful or chewing

each mouthful of food so many times. Interrupt eating with pauses, and make the meal a social event rather than a will of filling your gut.

The behavior modification program also includes education in nutrition, learning what foods to eat and learning the caloric value of foods. It emphasizes calorie counting and physical exercise. It suggests you avoid telling yourself, *I have no will power, I'll always be fat, What's the point of trying?* These negative messages just lead to more eating in an attempt to comfort yourself.

Aim for short-term goals, Dr. Stunkard seems to suggest. Pick a desired weight loss for only one or two weeks ahead and concentrate on changing the way you behave, because only when you change that will the weight come off and stay off. Also don't use sweeping generalities such as *I can never eat sweets again!* Instead do what Stacy did, the young woman I talked about in the beginning of this chapter. She said, "I limited my sweets to one frozen yogurt pop a week and included its calories in my diet." And finally, always think of how much weight you lost, not how much you still have to lose. As one successful dieter told me, "I could say I only lost five pounds, and I've got so much more to take off, but I prefer to say, I've already lost five pounds. What a great start!"

Reward is an important factor in behavior modification, and a very good reward is how nice you look after the weight is off as well as the praise and admiration of your friends and family. But a reward for dieting can also be the excellent health the dieter feels, the spring to the step that comes as that load of fat melts away.

"Do you realize," Stacy told me when she had dieted down to the weight she was aiming at, "I have carried an extra load of seventy-five pounds around with me for the last ten years. Do you know what that has done to my heart and back? Try it sometime. Pick up twenty-five pounds of rocks, strap them to your back and walk around with them!" She shook her head. "What a fool I've been for not starting sooner! How many years I've missed this wonderful feeling of freedom."

What fools we all are for carrying that excess poundage around, but then where is it written, in what book of wisdom, that men and women are not foolish? Foolishness is very much a part of the human condition, along with love and selfishness and wisdom and brutality and tenderness. We are all human, and it is pointless to dwell on our foolishness. Instead, consider the tremendous ability to change and adapt that all humans have. We can lose any amount of weight, even when we've carried it around for years and years. With all our foolishness, selfishness, brutality, even with our love and tenderness and wisdom, the one magnificent quality that we have is that ability to change. At any point in our lives we are capable of starting over again in a totally new direction. Even fat people, no matter at what age, can begin again and diet away those excess pounds. Try doing it. You might like it.

# 8

# THE EXERCISE ALTERNATIVE

### Eighteen Raw Clams

When he was halfway through the FATAWAY diet, Barry, another old friend, called me up and said, "Let's have lunch together. I have a problem."

"Eating out on the diet is tricky . . . " I began, but Barry cut me off.

"No sweat. I know this fantastic Japanese sushi place."

"What about all that rice?"

"I order sashimi. That's the raw fish sliced on top of a bowl of rice. I eat the fish without the rice. It's a little heavy on the protein, but I make up for it with a vegetable dinner."

We met, and the sushi and sashimi were all that Barry promised. "What's the problem?" I asked as we sipped our green tea.

"It's the diet."

"You're still on it?"

"Oh yes, and the weight is coming off. I feel good, but—I don't feel satisfied in terms of food. I mean, maybe I've got an oral streak and need to eat more. I don't know. I just wish I could run the diet up another thousand calories and lose weight. Or is that impossible?"

I considered the question carefully while I dipped the last piece of raw tuna into soy sauce and savored its taste. "Well, there is a way you could do it.''

"You mean eat more and still lose weight?'' Barry asked eagerly. "You've heard about some new pill, huh? Something like that stuff Muhammad Ali allegedly took to lose all that weight before his fight with Larry Holmes.''

"Thyroid? Heaven forbid! Sure, thyroid will speed up your metabolism and make you burn up food and fat at a faster rate, but it will also play hell with your body. You saw what it did to Ali. He lost the damned fight. No, no pill, no medicine. There's no magic cure-all for weight loss. All those diet pills you see advertised are either phoneys or dangerous. You know, amphetamines were first marketed as a sort of psychic energizer, a pill designed to pep you up. The trouble was, they also took away the appetite. The smart drug companies turned that side effect into a virtue. They marketed them as appetite suppressants! They're what the kids call *speed,* and they're damned easy to get hooked on.'' I shook my head. "Come on, Barry. You have to face the fact that whatever you eat you either burn up in energy or store as fat. Eat less, store less. Eat less than that, and you'll lose your storage.''

Barry patted his stomach. "I know. This extra baggage I'm carrying around my waist.'' He laughed. "But you said there was a way.''

"Oh, yes, if there's a will there's always a way. Now get this scenario. This is your life, Barry. You get up at seven, breakfast, then your wife drives you to the train station . . . ''

"Sometimes I drive myself in our extra jalopy,'' he put in. "And that takes a lot of energy, just getting the old wreck started.''

"Big deal. So you head into the city reading your paper on the train. Work all morning, lunch at your desk . . . "

"Sometimes on a park bench."

"Then you work all afternoon, the train home and dinner, play with the kids, TV, a movie or a book, and so to bed."

"Come on," Barry put in impatiently, "spare me the lifestyle bit, and tell me how I can eat more and still lose weight."

"There's only one way. Change your lifestyle and get out of the sedentary rut you're in."

Barry shrugged. "How? By running around the block on my lunch hour?"

"It's not a bad idea. Do you realize that twenty minutes of running burns up almost four hundred calories?"

"Four hundred calories?" He sat back, surprised, and stared at me over the table. "Four hundred calories is, let's see . . . " He began to grin as he took his handy pocket calorie counter out of his jacket. "Four hundred calories, here, one serving of spaghetti with sauce, or—hey—a piece of strawberry short cake! And look at this. Two slices of pizza pie at a hundred and sixty calories each. I'd have eighty calories left over."

"Now you've got it. If you could run each day for twenty minutes, you could add any of those to your FATAWAY diet and still lose weight."

"Yeah, but twenty minutes . . . I have a pretty full schedule. Frankly, I don't know how I could fit in an extra twenty minutes."

"Everyone has a full day. Let me run this past you. Say you get up half an hour earlier, and before breakfast you go out and do your twenty minutes of running. How does that grab you?"

"It doesn't." He sighed. "The timing is lousy. I hate to get up that early, and there's no decent place to run near my house."

"Okay, let's put running aside. Could you spare ten minutes in the morning?" When he nodded, I said, "How far are you from the railroad station?"

"Oh, about a mile. I get the drift. I could walk to the station. That takes about ten minutes. How many calories?"

"Well, it's not as good as running, but ten minutes of brisk walking burns up fifty calories. Ten minutes of running burns up two hundred. But say you walk to the station in the morning and home at night. That's a hundred calories. Then at your lunch hour, eat your lunch at your desk or on a park bench and walk the rest of the hour. Let's say you get in forty minutes of walking. That's another two hundred calories. What would three hundred calories buy you?"

Barry thumbed through his calorie counter. "Eighteen raw clams! I love clams, but I don't think I could handle that many. Let's see, three boiled potatoes. That would fill out dinner. Or two doughnuts, now that's speaking my language. An ice cream cone. Pity to waste three hundred on that. Hey, look at this. I could have six strips of bacon with my eggs in the morning. I like that."

"Well, you can take it from there. Get your bicycle out on Saturday. An hour's riding will buy you over four hundred calories, or jog over to the local high school and use their pool. Ten minutes of swimming gets you over a hundred calories."

## The Energy Equivalents

When I left Barry, I gave him the following list of energy equivalents. It details the number of calories you spend doing some typical exercises—walking, bike riding, swimming and running:

| The food you can have | Number of minutes | | | | |
|---|---|---|---|---|---|
| | The calories spent | walking | biking | swimming | running |
| One gingersnap or<br>One raw carrot | 20 | 4 | 2 | 2* | 1 |
| 1/2 cup fresh strawberries | 30 | 6 | 4 | 3 | 2 |
| One large fresh peach | 50 | 10 | 6 | 4 | 3 |
| One hard roll | 100 | 19 | 12 | 9 | 5 |
| Three ounces sweet sherry | 150 | 29 | 18 | 13 | 8 |
| One slice boiled ham | 200 | 38 | 24 | 18 | 10 |
| Two eggs scrambled in butter | 250 | 48 | 30 | 22 | 13 |
| Three ounces of sirloin steak<br>or<br>One-half cup canned tuna in oil | 300 | 57 | 36 | 27 | 15 |
| Two inch square of chocolate layer cake | 350 | 67 | 42 | 31 | 18 |
| One serving of strawberry shortcake, biscuit type, with cream | 400 | 77 | 49 | 36 | 21 |
| One chocolate malted milk shake | 500 | 97 | 61 | 45 | 26 |

As I had told Barry, the principle of the conservation of calories applies. Any healthy person can increase the amount of exercise done in a day to either lose weight faster or increase the amount of food on his diet. Is it worth it?

When I suggested it for Barry, it worked. He

* At these low amounts, it's hard to get a very accurate count. Biking does use up more energy than swimming, as you can see from the rest of the table.

took me up eagerly and added walking to his daily schedule, plus some biking with his son on Saturday. The combined calories spent in both exercises allowed him to expand his diet so that he could include those foods he had been missing so much, and he could still lose weight. But when I suggested the same approach to another friend— Sally, who was on the same diet—she shook her head. "No, it's just not worth it."

"What do you mean?"

"I'm a sedentary person. My idea of exercise is turning the pages of a good book. That's my nature. But I don't like putting on weight, and I'm determined to take this fat off, so I'll have to do it by counting calories." (Incidentally, Sally stuck to her diet and her fat did come off.)

"You still count calories when you exercise."

"Perhaps, but to me it's counting them the hard way. I don't like to run or bike or swim, and I'm too fond of my little sports car to walk. I don't like exercise, period. I can't stand all those jogging nuts who fill the streets. Would you believe I saw one running up Madison Avenue in all that auto exhaust? Crazy! No, I'm not about to do it, nor will I play tennis or roller skate. Boring! I'll make it my own way. I don't mind giving up the extra food. If that's what it takes to get slim again, I'll go that route."

The trouble was, Sally thought of exercise only in terms of calories spent. There is a great deal more benefit from exercise than just losing weight. There are both psychological and physiological benefits to the mind and the body, not only in terms of muscle tone but also in terms of our total health.

One of the first questions to answer when it

comes to exercise, is what sort is best for me; that is, assuming you're not like Sally who couldn't cotton to any physical activity. In specific terms, the answer to this depends on you yourself, on what you enjoy most or what is most convenient. But in more general terms, we can compare one type of exercise with another and decide which is best for us.

## *Beau and the Lady Weightlifter*

My friend Beau was an indirect victim of the wrong kind of exercise. I ran into him one afternoon in a coffee shop in Greenwich Village. There is something about Beau that always makes me feel a bit sad. He's a born loser. This time Beau's right leg was in one enormous cast from hip to ankle.

"Skiing?" I asked uncertainly. I couldn't imagine Beau on the slopes. He was your everyday basic urban cowboy, over thirty, perpetually single and perpetually trying to score.

"Sit down and have a cuppa coffee," he said. "How've you been?"

"Your leg?" I asked, easing into the chair across the table. "What happened?"

He sighed deeply. "Would you believe an affair of the heart?"

"You'd better tell me from the beginning," I said. With Beau you never knew what to expect.

"There's not much to tell. It was this girl I met at Maxwell's Plum," he began, wincing as he leaned back. "You wouldn't believe her." He made a vaguely flattering, vaguely obscene gesture. "Anyway, I was overwhelmed by her, and in no time it was 'your place or mine.' We decided on hers, and once we got there, I came on strong, the real macho bit.'' When I looked dubious, he shrugged. "Well, I read this book that says every woman likes a little of the rough stuff, so I tried it.'' He shook his head. "You wouldn't believe what happened next. It was incredible. I made a grab for her, and pow! I'm on the floor in agony.''

My mouth fell open. "She broke your leg? What was she? A black belt in karate or a lady wrestler?''

"Hell no, neither. In fact, the funny thing is, she didn't mind my coming on strong.''

I was genuinely puzzled. "Let me sort this out because I still don't understand about your leg. This woman was willing, and you put the move on her. Seems to me there shouldn't have been any problem.''

"Believe me, there was a problem. This lady's bible was some book on weightlifting for women by a guy named Arnold something. She follows it religiously and works out every day.''

"I'm beginning to see. She was too strong for you. She broke your leg.''

"Hell no! It wasn't like that. The thing is, she had a body that was hard as a rock. I made a grab, slipped and slammed up against her with my leg. Zap! That did it.''

When I stopped laughing about two days later, I realized that poor Beau was the victim of the woman's overdeveloped body. Still, I found it hard to believe that he had fractured his leg against his lady friend's hard muscles. More likely, I figured, it was a collision with the bed or the floor. Beau never was well coordinated. But he swore up and down that his pickup's muscles had done him in.

"That chick was built like a brick wall—literally!''

I tracked down Beau's vague reference on working out and weightlifting women, and found that the book was a slim volume with the author's photo on the back cover. He was a peculiarly proportioned man who would have made Superman slink back into his phone booth in dismay. Enormous muscles covered with writhing snakes of veins seemed to me grotesque and useless. I've known fine athletes with tremendous skill and endurance, and all of them had normally muscled bodies, smooth and pleasant to the eye. Did this weightlifter intended to force women into the same grotesque mold in which he had cast himself?

Indeed he did, and his book was a blueprint for accomplishing it. Linking muscular development to the woman's liberation movement, he had been holding seminars on weightlifting for women. While admitting, thank heaven, that women did not have the hormonal makeup that allows muscles to swell to great proportions, he pointed out that they could still expand their rib cages, build up the pectoral muscles that support their breasts, expand their thighs and arms and in general harden and shape up their bodies.

Now I have as much respect as the next man for a shapely, rounded woman, but I couldn't make up my mind about a ''hardened'' woman who had developed her body with what this weightlifter called ''resistance training.''

Resistance training, I discovered after a little research, is what weightlifting is all about, and it is a first cousin to isometrics. Isometrics started in the 1950s when it was discovered that pushing against something that did not move was only partly a waste of time. Do it once a day for only six seconds and you increase your muscle strength by 5 percent.

The basic principles behind isometrics are over-loading the muscles, depleting your oxygen supply and forcing them to rebuild themselves. Done properly, it can improve the strength of the tendons and ligaments and the overall body structure.

You can do isometric exercises by pushing against yourself, hand against hand, or by pushing against a desk—an easy way to exercise at work. While this will build muscles, it won't take off weight. For that you must push against the table before each meal is finished.

By the end of the 1970s, isometrics had fallen by the wayside, and the fickle public was searching for something new in the body business. Weightlifting, which had been around for a long time, stepped into the gap. It introduced resistance exercises. Unlike isometrics, resistance exercise allows you to move that object you are straining against, whether it's a dumbbell, a barbell or an intricate machine. You can move it, but not very far, and it takes a great deal of strain. Weightlifting also allows you to force almost any muscle of your body into oxygen depletion and subsequent rebuilding. If you stick with it, you can become as muscle-bound as the Incredible Hulk or Beau's "brick-wall chick."

I wouldn't ever knock exercise, and both iso-metrics and weightlifting are forms of exercise, but are these forms as good for you as running around the block? Outside of the cosmetic angle, and I'm not at all sure that women or men look all that beautiful with bulging muscles, is there a sound health reason for weightlifting? Will the musculature you achieve with weights and machines do what the weightlifters say it will? Will it help you "bear the pressures of the worlds of business, industry and government," as one book on the subject puts it, and will it "improve your health and decrease your chance of a heart attack, make you alert and less frustrated and better able to function in a highly competitive world," as another book insists?

## Responding to Exercise

There are claims that books on weightlifting make, and to check them out, I spoke to a friend, an internist who is heavily involved in sports medicine and has a neatly lettered motto over his office door. SHAPE UP OR SHIP OUT!

"I bought it in an army surplus store," he told me, grinning at it fondly. "It doesn't completely apply, but it's close enough. I give my overweight patients the choice of knocking off their excess poundage or finding another doctor."

"What I want to talk about," I told him, "is not weight loss, but exercise. And I want to ask you about weightlifting. I know it builds muscles, but is it good for you?"

"Sure it's good—if you want big muscles . . . " he began, but I interrupted.

"Be serious. I've read that it will decrease your chance of having a heart attack, or at least improve your chances of recovery if you do have one."

"You're on the wrong track. Let me explain a basic fact to you. Weightlifting builds muscles, but it is of no significant benefit to the body core. Should I repeat that? It bears repeating."

133

I stopped him just in time. "Tell me what you mean by the *body core.*"

"It's the heart, the lungs, the circulation. Weightlifting, resistance exercises, isometrics . . . they all build muscles, but they don't increase endurance. Working out with these methods give you none of the benefits you get from, say running, or a good game of tennis, squash or basketball. Do any of these on a regular basis, or swim or ride a bicycle, or for that matter, walk. I'll tell you, walk about four miles in an hour four times a week and your body core—all right, your lungs, heart and circulation—will all improve. That's the kind of muscle work-out that makes sense. Forget about those stationary exercises where you lift weights in a gym to build a better body. You know, your body responds to the kind of exercise you give it."

"What do you mean by that?" I asked uncertainly.

"Well . . ." He frowned. "It's simple. If you run, the muscles you use in running develop, and you become a better runner. If you play a team sport, you become a better team player as you practice. Whatever the activity, the appropriate muscles develop to make that activity easier. In endurance sports, running, swimming, basketball, walking—anything like that—your heart has to pump harder and your circulatory system improves. Less cholesterol is deposited on the blood-vessel walls and there's less chance of a heart attack. Your endurance increases, your brain is clearer and even your psychological outlook improves."

"And with weightlifting?"

"There you are. Practice weightlifting and you become a better weightlifter. You are able to lift heavier and heavier weights. But even so, you must be careful. I wouldn't recommend weightlifting to anyone with circulatory problems, but I would recommend a program of jogging or running."

"Why is that?"

"For one thing, blood pressure rises abruptly when a weight is lifted. That puts a strain on the heart and circulatory system. We don't want to strain those systems. We want a gradual adaptation to increased use."

"I get it."

"I hope so. There are some other points you should get," my doctor friend said earnestly. "I know that weightlifting is recommended for all ages and both sexes, but our bodies play funny tricks on us as we get older. Someone with arthritis or bursitis or tendonitis can be badly hurt by weightlifting."

"So you wouldn't advise it at all."

"Hold on. Now that I've told you some of the bad angles, let me point out a few goodies. You can fill out your shoulders, your calves, your arms or thighs with selected weightlifting—if that's what you want to do. For a man, it looks good in the locker room."

"And for a woman?"

He shrugged. "Depends on how feminine she wants to be—or how tough and strong."

I thought of Beau's fractured leg. "I've always thought soft and round was womanly."

"You're a typical male chauvinist pig," my friend said with pleasant satisfaction. "Womanly is whatever the culture says it is. In the Victorian days it was a tiny waist and big hips and breasts. In the '20s it was flat, flat, flat! Now it's trim and slim, nicely rounded but not bulgy. Me, I'm a runner and there's nothing as pleasant as pacing a well-built young woman—about five yards behind and watching the smooth muscular coordination of her body . . . "

I looked at him with raised eyebrows. "Why, you're a dirty young man!"

"Why not?" He smiled pleasantly. "Why not?"

A good deal of follow-up research as well as some serious talks with a number of other medical men convinced me that he was right about exercise. A sad thing about our civilization is that it tends to make us so sedentary. Most white collar workers or factory workers do jobs that require very little exercise. While they may become mentally exhausted and translate that into physical fatigue, their bodies are severely underworked. Many are aware of this but seem helpless in the face of the tendency to become flabby and overweight as they grow older.

Men and women who do manage to remain active into their adult years, who jog or swim or run or play tennis or squash or any of the other popular sports, do it not so much for health reasons, but simply because it feels good and they consider it fun, or else it is the "in" thing to do.

Whatever the reasons for continuing exercise into adult life, it is not only fun and games, but it is also good for health and can prolong life and improve the quality of life.

The risk of heart disease, we all know, drops in proportion to a person's physical activity. This is because physical activity increases the heart's ability to pump blood and improves the circulation. The body tissues get more oxygen, and even the coronary arteries, those blood vessels that feed the heart, are larger and more open in physically active people. Their blood pressure is lower and their hearts beat more regularly.

There is a blood substance that carries cholesterol, and it's called *High Density Lipids* (HDL). As near as researchers can tell, this substance protects us against heart attacks. In fact, we can anticipate the likelihood of a heart attack by the level of HDL in our blood. The higher it is, the less chance of an attack. Athletes have very high levels of HDL; sedentary people have low levels. It seems tied to the amount of exercise you do. Increase your exercise and your HDL level goes up—and the risk of a heart attack goes down.

The heart isn't the only part of the body that benefits from exercise. Exercise makes us more sensitive to insulin. If diabetics exercise, they can often get along on smaller amounts of insulin. Of course exercise burns up calories and helps keep our weight down. It also keeps our bones from losing calcium. Older people often develop a condition called osteoporosis, in which the bones become weak and fracture easily because of a calcium loss. Exercise can slow down this loss.

While the body benefits from exercise in one direction, the mind benefits in another. Anxiety, depression and tension are all relieved by exercise. Dr. Edward D. Greenwood, Psychiatrist at the Menninger Clinic, believes that a constant program of exercise will "enhance ego strength, dissipate anger and hostility, relieve boredom and resolve frustration."

Strong words, but encouraging ones. Anyone interested in improving his health, inside and out, should consider exercise very seriously. If you're under thirty, don't hesitate, but build up gradually. Never start at your peak performance no matter

137

what your age. Start slowly and build up a bit more each day. Never allow yourself to become exhausted. Work up the point of tiredness and then stop. Gradually you'll reach your pattern of maximum performance.

If you are over thirty and you've never been one to exercise, get a medical checkup before you start. There are some illnesses that just don't go with exercise. Check it out.

# 9

## WOMEN AND EXERCISE

### Women's Muscles

Susan was one of the successful dieters on my FATAWAY program, but like my friend Barry she felt the need of something else. "I've always had this terrible sweet tooth. Sometimes I feel I could kill for two scoops of coffee ice cream!"

"That bad?" I laughed and then explained to her, as I had to Barry, the principle of the exercise alternative.

Susan's eyes lit up. "I'd gladly exercise twenty minutes to get my ice-cream fix. As a matter of fact, I've been seriously thinking of tennis. I used to be good at it in high school and Harold, my boy friend, is really into it. Hey, you know, we could go away for tennis weekends. What a gas!"

Susan picked up a couple of snappy little tennis outfits and began practicing in secret to surprise Harold. "He'll flip out when I take him on!"

Between her secret tennis sessions and her diet, her weight began to come off and her entire body firmed up. "It's just beautiful," she told me enthusiastically. "Especially when I get out on the court and work up a good, healthy sweat. I feel just great, and it turns out I'm some fantastic player. Is Harold going to be in for a shock! But isn't it crazy I should work so hard at tennis and feel so good? And still get my ice-cream fix!"

But a month later when I met Susan, her enthusiasm was all gone. "What happened? No luck in the tournament?"

"Oh no, it's Harold. He made me quit."

"What?" I was shocked. "Why would he do that?"

"Well, he doesn't think all this exercise is good for me. He says women are built differently, and he for one wants them to stay that way. He says he wants his broad to be broad where a broad should be broad."

"Susie, you've got yourself a male chauvinist pig! These aren't the dark ages." I shook my head. "You should do what *you* think is right."

"Well, that's just the trouble. I think he may be right. I don't want to get that bulky, athlete look. Hey, the last thing I want is to be a musclewoman. The next thing I know I'll have to start shaving!"

"Hold off on the shaving cream for a while," I told her, and I began to do a little research on my own. I'm a runner myself, and I've always admired the slim, well-built women who trot past me on the Central Park Reservoir track. Slim they were, and nicely put together, but there didn't seem to be any bulging muscles among them.

Now I know of a gym downtown that caters to women who are into weightlifting. If anything would develop unsightly muscles in women, it would be resistance exercise or weightlifting. I remembered my friend Beau and his weight-lifter pickup. She was as hard as nails, he had said, but she also had "some build" as Beau put it. There had been no mention of bulging muscles.

I took an afternoon off and went down to talk to some of the women at the gym and watch them work out. As I mentioned before, weightlifting does nothing good for the heart or body, but it

140

does develop muscles.

I was impressed with the women's ability to lift weights, but I was even more impressed with their bodies. There were none of the distorted muscles you find in male weightlifters. They were pleasantly rounded and very attractive. Barbara, who was quite willing to talk about her weight-lifting experience, told me she had been athletic all her life.

"This whole business of athletics and exercise masculinizing women is something we all dread. And it's not only a fear of what can happen to us physically, but also what can happen psychologically. Myself, I'm very much a woman, very feminine, and the idea of becoming thick and bulgy always bothered me. I never dared try weightlifting before, and in the other sports I used to lean over backwards and wear fussy outfits—I once put lace around the bottom of my running shorts! I would never cut my hair short, as convenient as it would have been." She shook her head. "Funny, I was probably twice as feminine as I'd ever have been without athletics, but it was just overreacting, a dread of being masculine. You know the old stereotype of the female Phys. Ed. teacher with the butch haircut and the hairy legs?"

I looked at her short, pretty hair and asked, "What changed you? What made you cut your hair and take up weightlifting?"

"The realization that all that physical activity wasn't giving me the bulging muscles I dreaded, nor did any of the women I knew who were into athletics change that much physically."

I found some justification for Barbara's views in a study done by two sociologists from Bowling Green State University, Eldon Snyder and Joseph Kivlin. They compared 275 undergraduate, nonathletic women with 328 who were extremely active in a variety of sports. They discovered that physical differences were slight. The athletes tended to be about one inch taller on the average and three pounds heavier. Nor did the researchers find any bulging muscles in their women athletes.

They found that the major change in the bodies of women athletes was a decrease in subcutaneous fat, the fat that lies just under the skin. For some reason, perhaps hormonal, the muscles of women become more effective and stronger with exercise, but do not develop as men's muscles do, even under the stress of weightlifting. My session with Barbara convinced me of that. Though an accomplished weightlifter, her body was extremely feminine. The muscles were there. You could feel them, but they were not obvious.

When I told Susan what I had found out, she drew a sigh of relief. "Hey, that's great. Now I feel better about the tennis tournament."

"I thought you quit tennis."

"I went back. The other girls talked me into it. They said I was too good to cop out."

"What about Harold?"

"That creep? I dropped him. Hey, you know why he didn't want me to play tennis, his real reason? He was off on those tennis weekends shacking up with some other 'broad.' He's a real male chauvinist pig!"

## The Inner Woman

One of the positive findings that emerged from sociologists Snyder and Kivlin's study was that women athletes had very good body images, much more so than nonathletic women. They had more energy and better health, and surprisingly, they felt every bit as feminine as their nonathletic sisters. Some, in fact, felt even more feminine.

These positive feelings about themselves are all the more startling in the face of the pressure female athletes are under to be more ladylike and to avoid masculine sports. A number of teachers of physical education at various colleges have spoken out about this problem, and a woman at an upstate New York college told me, "It's a damned shame that even today, in this enlightened age of feminine awareness, women are being pushed into 'feminine' roles in sports."

When I asked her just what she meant, she said, "Even the Olympics forbids women to participate in certain sports. You know, any sport with direct body contact is frowned on for women. We're encouraged to be graceful and feminine, to go for skill rather than strength, and we're told that our bodies should move flowingly, Grecian style. In other words, what it all boils down to is that we should look good to men. How good can a woman look in a football scrimmage? So football is out. We're discouraged from participating in basketball or soccer and encouraged to stick with tennis, swimming and gymnastics. I'm surprised they don't still want us to dress in flowing robes and have us do turn-of-the-century calisthenics!"

But while the male-dominated sports world may resist the image of women in hard-hitting contact sports, women themselves, even those who aren't athletic, seem to find nothing wrong with tougher games. A study at Arizona State University by three researchers, Joan Kinglsey, a professor of physical education, Foster L. Brown, a psychologist, and Margaret Siebert, a doctoral student, concluded that college women find it completely acceptable to go in for relatively rough sports. They attached no social stigma to the female athlete.

What the female athlete feels about her own participation in sports is a little different. There seems to be, according to Snyder and Kivlin, a vague sense of guilt in female athletes, an apologetic attitude about their involvement in sports.

In an attempt to get some idea of the emotions women felt when they engaged in exercise, I questioned over a hundred women who were active in either exercise or sports. The majority were runners, but there were some basketball players, softball players, gymnasts and even one hockey player among them. The hockey player told me she gave up the game when she came close to getting her front teeth knocked out.

"It was at college," Selma told me, "and I was the only girl in the group. It wasn't the real school team, just 'jungle' hockey, and I felt pretty high the first time I checked a guy. I was good, and I could handle the roughness too. I was just afraid of getting scarred up, otherwise I would have kept on, maybe even tried out for the school team, struck a blow for women's rights!"

Her "high" during the games was echoed by the other active women I talked to. In describing their sports experience, they used terms such as *joy, cheerfulness, a sense of my own body and the bodies of others, a body language commitment during the game that made me feel real close to my teammates, a sense of beauty in the motion of the other runners, an exhilarating high.*

It went on like that, and I was struck by the sense of confidence and well-being almost all of these women felt. My random questionnaire seemed to agree with the findings of the large study by Snyder and Kivlin. These two researchers found that competitive athletics fosters a general sense of confidence and well-being. The athletes they interviewed generally felt "in good spirits," "very satisfied with life," and found "much happiness in life."

Other studies indicate that sports can breed self-confidence and a sense of identity in women, especially in adolescents. However, there is always the possibility in analyzing the results of such studies that the women who were self-confident and had a strong, positive sense of their own identity were the ones who went in for athletics.

Whichever came first, the strong sense of self, or the participation in athletics, it is increasingly evident from all these studies that women do not lose by becoming athletes. The criticism that it lessens their femininity is as invalid as the criticism that asking for equal rights "defeminizes" a woman. This argument was used when working women in the garment trades and in factories went out on strike, and when women began demonstrating for suffrage. Such aggressive actions were considered defeminizing. No one suggested that women in sweat shops or factories were defeminized by the hard demanding work they did.

"I used to think that women were built differently from men in a structural sense," a male high-school athletic coach told me. "All the books said so, and they also said that was why women threw balls so awkwardly and ran in such a funny way."

Puzzled, I asked him, "What do you mean by *funny?*"

"Well, I'm an addicted watcher of TV's 'Charlie's Angels,' and I always crack up when I see those three women, supposedly graduates of a police academy, run in such an awkward, clumsy way. Watch the program sometime, and you'll see what I mean. They hold their arms peculiarly, and their entire body stance is—well, the only word I can think of is girlish."

"You said that you *used* to think that. Obviously something has changed your mind about the way women are built, and just as obviously it isn't one of Charlie's Angels."

"I'm a runner, a serious runner. I've finished the Boston Marathon three years in a row. Now when I'm out running these days, there are a lot of women on the track, and I've watched them over the past years. You know what I think?"

"No. Tell me."

"I think all that talk about women being built differently is baloney. I mean in terms of how their arms and legs are joined. In the beginning some years ago when only a few women were out running, you could see that 'Charlie's Angels Syndrome,' that awkward arm movement and body wiggle. Now I'd say 80 percent of the women run the way men do. They hold their arms the same way. Their stride is the same, and they're good—

damn good.''

"What changed them?''

"They forgot they were women, and they began to run naturally. Men, women, hell—there's an sexlessness to athletics, or there should be. Sure men have stronger muscles than women, and they're built bigger. But I can't see any reason they shouldn't compete, if not together, then at least at the same sports.''

I found this suggestion of androgyny echoed by Carole Oglesby, associate professor of sports psychology at Temple University. In a book she has edited, *Women and Sport: From Myth to Reality,* she says "sport is neither masculinity training nor femininity training, but androgyny training.''

Sports, she points out, "can assist the development of independence and domination (two qualities of the so-called masculine principle).'' But it can also assist in developing qualities such as dependence and subordination, usually held to be feminine. In baseball, for example, "in the many sacrifice situations (and in scores of other instances) a player learns the benefits of subordination of personal glory to team victory.''

In sports, and in exercise in general, the dividing line between men and women seems to become thinner and thinner, and someday it may disappear altogether. Does this mean we should someday expect to see pro-football teams with women linebackers? I doubt it very much. Professional football is in a different category, a money-making venture, and even good male players don't stand a chance unless they're top-of-the-heap. But the breakthrough of women into sports is not concerned with coed participation in professional athletics that are now strictly the male province:

soccer, baseball, football. It is in grade school, high school and even college that mixed teams will teach young women self-confidence, leadership ability and the strength to fight for the causes they believe in. It will give them a chance to question society's more rigid sex roles. This can be good or bad, depending on whether you believe women should or shouldn't be emancipated.

In a recent article in *Psychology Today*, Joanna Bunker Rohrbaugh, of the department of psychiatry at Harvard Medical School and Massachusetts General Hospital, notes that "when we stop seeing the world in terms of male athletes and female cheerleaders, we may also stop experiencing it in terms of male tyrants and female subordinates, male wifebeaters and female victims, male achievers and female admirers."

Of course, all of this is grist for tomorrow's mills. Today, for most women, it's not a struggle to enter competitive sports with men, but a struggle to overcome the years of conditioning that have taught them that exercise is not ladylike, and if they do exercise, it should be in a graceful manner pleasing to the eye, that is to the male eye.

Am I setting up a straw man? Surely this type of conditioning is Victorian and should have been discarded at the end of the Victorian era. The sad truth is that shreds of such thinking still engulf us. Dorothy Harn, of the department of physical education at Pennsylvania State University, writes that a woman tennis player takes a risk when she wins a tennis match from a man or "outperforms any male whether it be in sports, business or any profession dominated by the male. Competitive sports are still the prerogative of the male in this society."

Undoubtedly it's true, and the woman who enters competitive sports must be aware of this risk and be prepared to face up to it. But this is also true for the woman who goes into business, or as Ms. Harn says, any area dominated by men!

### Steam or Sauna

"You can talk to me all you want about the fact that exercise doesn't defeminize a woman," Helen told me, "but the fact remains that somewhere, deep in my feminine psyche, there is a virulent anathema to exercise. Am I using the word anathema correctly?"

I looked at Helen's sleek, trim body with admiration. "However you use the word, you must be doing something right. You look great. If exercise is such a problem for you, how do you manage to do it?"

"I don't do it. I keep my figure with steam baths and sauna. I belong to a health club, but I don't use the gym. I go at least three times a week, and I alternate between the sauna and the steam room. One gives me dry heat, and the other moist heat, and the combination of the two is terrific. I sweat off all my excess weight, and I get rid of the poisons in my system. I call it my hot road to health."

"I'm afraid," I said tentatively, "that you're kidding yourself. I can't believe that a steam room or sauna has helped you take off weight. I know that it just doesn't work that way."

Helen shrugged an elegant shoulder. "Whatever you know, I'm telling you what it does for me. It takes off the weight. How else would I keep this way?"

"Do you diet at all?" I asked.

"At all?" Helen laughed. "My dear man, my life is one huge diet. Eternal vigilance is the price of a good figure. I haven't touched sweets in so long, I've forgotten what they taste like."

"But I've had dinner with you, and you seem to eat normally."

"Oh, I've got my little tricks to keep it from being obvious. I'll tell you, darling, there's nothing that bores people as much as letting them know you're dieting. I diet in private. I have coffee and juice for breakfast, a salad and fruit for lunch and a simple dinner, meat or fish and a vegetable. Then, if I eat out I have a normal meal. I even allow myself a roll and a pat of butter in a restaurant. Coffee, but no dessert. Secret dieting, and most important of all, I get my steam and sauna regularly."

I didn't probe any further into Helen's technique for staying fit. I was positive that it was her dieting alone that kept the excess weight off. The steam and sauna simply answered some sensual need. I can understand that, for while I dislike the dry heat of a sauna, I revel in moist steam. I like to stretch out my muscles with a long swim and then relax in the soothing warmth of a steam room, but I have friends who say the same thing about a sauna. It's a matter of taste, but the truth is that neither of the two do the slightest good in terms of weight loss.

Dry or moist heat will cause you to sweat

copiously and lose a lot of water. Step on a scale afterwards and indeed you weigh less, but this weight loss is not real. After a few drinks of water, the body rehydrates itself, and your weight returns to what it was before. There's no way either type of heat can burn away fat.

Of the two, I prefer steam, but the fact is steam heat can be dangerous, and the sauna is the safer of the two. To understand why, consider what sweating does to the body. Sweating is a technique the body uses for cooling off. The body picks up heat in a number of ways, through cell and muscle action, from the metabolism of food and from the environment. When you exercise, you heat up your body very rapidly, and it becomes necessary to lose some of that heat. Sweating films the skin with a fine layer of moisture. As that moisture evaporates, it cools the skin. The blood flowing through the very small vessels near the skin is also cooled, and it returns to cool the body by picking up excess heat. It's a fine cooling system, but it requires two things. The ability to sweat, and the opportunity for the sweat to evaporate.

In a hot, dry environment such as a sauna, we sweat a great deal, and the sweat can evaporate and cool us down. We receive heat from the sauna, but we lose it as our sweat evaporates into the dry air. In a very humid environment, such as a steam room, sweating goes on, but losing that sweat through evaporation is difficult. There is too much moisture in the air. Instead, the sweat rolls off us. In this kind of situation, the body heat can easily rise to dangerous levels, and heat exhaustion can occur.

If you go into a steam room after a heavy workout in a gym, you compound the problem. The body heat has been raised by the exercise, and you need to lose that heat. The steam prevents heat loss.

So on the whole, if you must have heat, you're safer in the sauna than in the steam room. But before you try either, you should be aware of some of the myths that surround them. The only advantage to a steam bath is psychological. It feels good, and to many people this is worth any risk involved. Most people who use steam rooms, however, are just not aware that they're taking a risk.

## Sweating It Out

As far as health goes, there is no benefit to be gotten from steam. You cannot steam away fat, and the only weight loss is water. Excess sweating, whether in a steam room or a sauna or after a heavy bout of exercise, is potentially dangerous not only because the body becomes overheated, but also because the sweating causes a loss of electrolytes, sodium, potassium and chloride. Losing both electrolytes and body water may eventually damage your kidneys.

The fluid and electrolytes can be replaced. A drink of orange juice, a banana or a heavy sprinkling of salt on your food will do it, and of course the lost fluid can be restored with a glass or two of water. The idea that sweating is good because it gets rid of body poisons, something I've heard many people repeat, is false. In fact too much sweating can cause the sweat glands to take energy away from other organs of the body.

Some people find wet or dry heat relaxing and even tranquilizing, but these forms of relaxation are psychological effects. I've known people who get the same effect from a sunset or autumn leaves or the right kind of music. Other people find the heat of steam or sauna beneficial to aches and pains in their muscles. And if they do, why not use them? But whatever a sauna may do for you, remember that what it does *not* do is help colds get better, clear up your skin, help arthritis or bursitis or increase overall fitness.

Old people and those with diabetes, heart disease or high blood pressure should avoid both steam rooms and saunas. If you are reasonably healthy and determined that you benefit from excess heat of some kind, then you should opt for the sauna. Make sure the temperature is not above 185 degrees Fahrenheit and the humidity is very low. Ten minutes should be the maximum for the first-time sauna user, and you should wait for two hours after eating before going into one. *Never* use it when you are drunk or on drugs, even prescription drugs unless you check it out with your doctor.

Lately another "guaranteed" weight-loss device has made its appearance. This is the rubberized belt, hip hugger or sweat suit. The theory is that using them will reduce the part of your body you cover. Like any other get-thin-quick scheme, they don't work. While measurements taken after their use will show a slight reduction of weight, an hour later the body springs back to normal. What has happened is that the covered area has shrunk temporarily because of the rubberized material's interference with sweating. There is no significant weight loss or size reduction, and there is always a danger that these gadgets may cause a dangerous rise in body temperature.

To sum up, heat can relax you and may be of some psychological benefit. If you feel that you really need it, try the dry heat instead of the wet. If, like me, you're hooked on steam in spite of its uselessness and danger, make sure you get enough fluids into your body, and don't steam up for too long. A cool shower will help get your body heat back down.

Most important, avoid both steam and sauna after exercise. When you do exercise, wear as little clothing as possible. Give nature a break and let your own sweat do its job by cooling you down.

The entire business of sweating goes beyond steam and sauna. A healthy body is a marvelously balanced piece of equipment, and it usually stays at an average temperature of about 99 degrees Fahrenheit. When you build up too much heat through exercise, or hot surroundings, your body goes into its act and sweats to cool down. When you're too cold, that same clever body conserves heat by keeping your blood away from the areas where it easily loses heat: the arms, legs and skin.

Avoid excess heat or cold when you exercise. Dress lightly and if you run, jog, play tennis or bike outdoors in the hot summer months, do it in the cool of morning or late evening. In the winter dress sensibly to avoid chills and beware of sucking in too much cold air. This can chill your lungs and be as deadly as too much heat. The big secret of exercise is to use your brain as well as your body.

# 10

## NO EASY WAY

### Pounding the Flesh

"You can advise diet and exercise all you want," Larry told me. "But I have a much better system for keeping fit and losing weight."

I was surprised at that, for I had never considered Larry to be in the "fit" category. In his late thirties, Larry was a successful Chicago businessman. He was something of a wheeler-dealer and an impeccable dresser. His expensive, hand-tailored suits minimized, but didn't really hide, his growing corporation. At a quick guess, Larry was at least thirty pounds overweight. "Your system may be better," I said doubtfully, "but I don't think it's working. What is it?"

"Massage," Larry said complacently. "And it hardly interrupts my day. I really am too busy for exercise, and as for dieting, hell there are days when all three of my meals are tied into business. Lunch is always with a client, and often dinner is too. My wife and I will wine and dine an out-of-town customer—and I've even had early breakfast meetings! That's to say nothing of the six-thirty drink to firm up a deal at the nearby bar. No, dieting is out of the question!"

"So you've substituted massage?"

"Right. My masseur comes to the office at five, and from five to six twice a week he gives me a full massage. It's fantastic."

"How did you get into massage?" I asked curiously.

Thoughtfully, Larry said, "It goes back to my first bad attack of low back pain. I had put on a lot of weight, and then very suddenly, I developed this bad back. The doctor wanted me to go through a whole mess of exercises, but I couldn't stick with them. I hadn't the patience nor the time. A friend of mine talked me into massage. I say talked me into because before that the idea of a stranger touching my body seemed an invasion of privacy. I went to his masseur with my friend, protesting all the way. I told him, 'The idea of some joker kneading and pounding me turns me off.'

"'What are you afraid of?' my friend asked. 'Why are you suddenly so uptight?'

"I couldn't really answer that, and my friend said, 'Look at it this way. Massage isn't a sexual act. Sure it's sensual, but basically it's a healing process. When I get a really good massage, it makes me feel complete, whole. I get a message from the masseur's hands, and my body gives out a message in return.' He finally convinced me, and I told his masseur about the pain in my back. The crazy thing was, he started by massaging my forehead." Larry smiled. "He was establishing a *liaison of touch*. I wanted to remind him that the pain was in my back, but I decided it was his job, and I'd mix out—let him do it his way.

"Now starting with my head that way eased my uneasiness about being touched. As he continued, his hands seemed to do more than massage," Larry shook his head. "Actually, he built up a rapport between us, a kind of body language that eased the tension out of my muscles as he worked on my stomach, arms and legs. When I turned over, and he finally reached my back, the spasm was much less than when he had started. By relaxing every other part of me first, he had relaxed my low back muscles too. By the time he started to work on them, I was almost without pain. When he was finished, I was like a new man. You know, ever since then I've had a massage regularly, and I've never had any more back pain! I feel like a million bucks afterwards, and what's more, I realize the massage is a good substitute for dieting."

"Up until that last sentence, I was with you," I laughed. "But there you lost me. Massage is relaxing, and it sure as hell will help any knotted muscles. But as a substitute for dieting? No way!"

"Well, you're wrong," Larry said firmly. "Massage is well known as a method of reducing. It breaks down the fat so that it can be carried away by the bloodstream. It demobilizes the fat cells. This is very important, especially in spot reducing. When it's properly done, massage can take fat off any specific spot, your hips, your thighs . . . "

## Lumps, Bumps and Bulges

Argue as I would, I couldn't shake Larry's firm conviction that massage was the ultimate answer for the exercise hater. Nor was he convinced by his own spreading girth that it didn't work. It was too easy to believe in massage, too comfortable a promise of weight control and too seductive a procedure. The pleasure of a good massage overcame any doubts about its efficiency.

157

I was surprised at Larry, but I shouldn't have been. I had gone through a similar but slightly different argument with Shirley, a cousin of mine in her early forties. Ten years after her divorce, Shirley had moved in with a young man of thirty. "Youth," she explained to me carefully, "is what you make it."

"I'm not quite sure I get that," I frowned.

"Well, I don't feel forty and Charles doesn't feel thirty. Age differences are a lot like sex differences. We've set up all these foolish conventions about women's roles and men's roles, and really, when you come down to it, it's a lot of play acting. We're human beings before we're men or women."

Slightly bewildered, I tried to sort it out. "You mean you're human beings rather than thirty or forty?"

"Exactly. So Charles is younger than I am. Big deal! As long as I feel young, who cares?" She hesitated and a slightly anxious look drew her brows together. " . . . and look young," she concluded weakly.

I didn't understand that last bit until a month later when we met by chance on the street and stepped into a nearby coffee shop to chat. "So how's the May-December romance?"

"Oh, don't tease me. We're doing very well . . . considering the circumstances."

"What circumstances?"

She shrugged. "This damned body of mine!"

"What's wrong with it?" I was genuinely puzzled. Shirley was a handsome woman and had kept her figure. Oh, perhaps a bit more of it than when she was young, but it all looked good to me and I told her so.

"That's because you can't see the cellulite," she

said broodingly.

"Cellulite!" I shook my head in disgust. "Now don't tell me you've fallen for that nonsense."

"It's not nonsense, as you'd realize if you could see my backside."

"It would be my pleasure."

"Don't be a smart-ass. I've got a date at a new spa today, and this is my last chance. But I'm sure it's going to work. They were trained by Ronsard and they do wrapping too."

"If you want to throw out your money . . . " I began, but Shirley cut me off.

"You scoff at everything, but I know this cellulite treatment works. I've seen women who look just wonderful afterwards. Besides, Charles wants me to try it."

So that was the trouble in paradise. I couldn't argue with it, and Shirley wasn't an isolated case. Recently the entire country was swept by the cellulite craze. A beauty salon owner, Nicole Ronsard, started it with a book titled, *Cellulite: Those Lumps, Bumps and Bulges You Couldn't Lose Before,* a long but catchy title. Ms. Ronsard maintains that a certain type of dimpled fat called *orange peel fat* is made up of a "gel-like substance consisting of fat, water and toxic waste trapped in lumpy, immovable pockets just beneath the skin."

Massaging these pockets, squirting them with high-pressure water along with a program of exercise, a special diet, sauna, laxatives and even diuretics, is the only method, according to Ms. Ronsard, of getting rid of cellulite.

Thousands of women, all over the country, have paid great sums of money to massage away their cellulite and look young again. My cousin Shirley was right in with the rest. When I saw her again, almost a year later, she was glowing. She and Charles were as happy as "two bugs in a rug!" Marriage? "No way," she told me disdainfully. "We're too mature for that, and we're both perfectly happy with things as they are."

"And your cellulite?"

"Well, look at me!" She put her hands on her hips and pivoted for me. While I couldn't see the lack of cellulite, I had to admit she looked sensational. "But you've been dieting and exercising too on the Ronsard program," I pointed out like a spoilsport. "I think that's what makes you look so great, not the cellulite treatment."

Her answer was a knowing sigh. "Men! You'll never understand."

Thinking of Larry and his massage, I wasn't so sure we men didn't understand, or at least weren't prey to the same foolish trap. Larry's conviction that massage could thin him down and Shirley's conviction that massage could get rid of her cellulite had a lot in common. The only difference was that Shirley had added diet and exercise to her program and that acted as a "fail-safe."

What Shirley could not accept is that there is no medical justification for the entire cellulite concept. No medical text on physiology or fat mentions it, and Dr. Philip L. White, director of the AMA's food and nutrition department, calls it a figment of Ms. Ronsard's imagination. But I must add it's a lucrative figment.

It's true that in some people fat is deposited in a dimpled way, but this is not cellulite. It is plain, old-fashioned fat, and all the massage in the world won't break it down. Yet the fantasy persists. There are still cellulite clinics that charge large fees, and there are still satisfied customers like Shirley who swear by the treatment, just as Larry swears by massage. The mere fact that a technique doesn't work is rarely discouraging. If it promises what you want, if it appeals to your fantasies, it will still be accepted.

## Shaking It Off

Dr. Millard E. Knapp, in an article on massage in the journal, *Postgraduate Medicine,* notes that massage will relieve pain, reduce swelling and mobilize contracted tissues. It may even benefit patients with arthritis and low back pain.

What it will not do is get rid of fat! Nor is it a practical alternative to exercise. Its main benefit is the relief of tension, and it should be accepted for just this very important service.

One offshoot of massage is the proliferation of all the machines so popular in gyms and health clubs that promise to shake away your surplus fat and exercise you without your doing the work. They contain vibration belts, rollers and a host of moving parts that knead and pound and twist and move the body while you passively submit. Like massage, they may make you feel good and relieve muscle spasms, but they will not take off weight and they cannot take the place of real exercise where you do the work yourself.

Drs. A.H. Steinhaus and V. Henlund, in the *Journal for the Association of Physical and Mental Rehabilitation,* stated, "the vibrator is not to be taken seriously as a device to assist in fat reduction or in shifting of fat deposits within the body." Fifteen minutes with a vibrator, the researchers find, would take off about one-twenty-third of an ounce of body fat. It would need a full year of its use for fifteen minutes every day to take off one pound of fat! You could save yourself a great deal of money and take off ten pounds in a year by walking for fifteen minutes every day!

## Yoga and Weight Loss

While I am going into some of the anti-exercise techniques that promise to take off weight and improve your vitality and endurance, I must mention Gerhardt and his yoga. As long as I've known Gerhardt, he has been intrigued with the philosophical, spiritual and physical disciplines of yoga. When Gerhardt comes to a party, you can be positive that within fifteen minutes he is down on the floor in a lotus position with a gaggle of eager disciples around him.

"Yoga," Gerhardt told me, "is a matter of getting into communion with the Superior Universal Spirit, or Paramatma. It helps me transcend profane existence."

But more than the spiritual aspects of yoga, Gerhardt would stress the physical and mental well-being that comes from its practice. "The rhythm of yoga is slow and precise," he once explained to me. "You don't exert yourself or stress yourself. The key is quiet, peace, concentration, meditation. That's why taking off weight with yoga is so good."

I was surprised. "I should think it's too slow an exercise program for weight loss. I can see its advantage in stretching muscles, but in weight

162

loss?''

''Oh yes,'' Gerhardt assured me. ''It will help you lose weight and actually trim inches off your body. It takes off the flab and firms you up. Now this is Hatha Yoga,'' he added at my dubious look. ''You know, Hatha Yoga is concerned with the development of the body. It aims at attaining good health and physical strength to endure the very rigorous other types of yoga. It's a step-by-step system of physical education that stresses the integration of the body as a whole through correct body posture and the strengthening and realignment of the muscles to reach unified balance. Have you ever read Hittleman on Yoga?''

I shook my head and Gerhardt explained. ''Richard Hittleman has written more on the subject than anyone else in America. He says that people who practice Hatha Yoga have improved flexibility, grace, serenity, relaxation, strength, alertness and clear heads. How about that?''

''It sounds impressive, and I might even buy it, but weight loss?''

Our argument didn't get very far, and I couldn't believe Gerhardt's claims, nor those of his authority, Richard Hittleman. I even read one of his many books, *Weight Control Through Yoga*, and I still had my doubts. I began to do some research on my own and discovered that in Hatha Yoga, the exercise recommended for weight reduction, two hundred to two hundred thirty calories are used up in an hour. Since the average yoga session is half an hour, we are talking about slightly more than a hundred calories.

Now just sitting and reading a book will burn up about fifty calories in half an hour. The total calorie loss of the yoga session is less than a good fifteen minute walk. In truth, it contributes almost nothing to weight loss and certainly nothing to help the cardiovascular system. As an exercise, Hatha Yoga is a dud. As a way of taking off flab, forget it. Perhaps it will firm up the body, though this is questionable. It certainly won't help your endurance.

The chief benefit of yoga is its calming effect. My friend Gerhardt is a very cool guy, perhaps a bit spaced-out, but then again, maybe only in communion with a higher consciousness. At any rate, I believe it's his spaced-out charm that leads to his success at parties. It's the magnet that attracts all those eager followers who try to copy his easy lotus position. All in all, yoga is a good way to relieve tension and stress. As with cellulite, I believe any weight reduction with yoga occurs because the people who are into it combine their exercises with a lactovegetarian diet and some degree of fasting. These, not the exercises, take off the weight.

### Let the Machine Do It for You

I can't leave this chapter on lazy exercisers without telling you about Joan and Teddy. They're a young married couple whose only exercise in the past ten years has been to produce a very large family.

"They keep me much too busy to even think of exercise," Teddy told his doctor as he buttoned up his shirt after his last medical examination. "Just earning enough to fill their darling little bellies occupies every minute of my day. I'm even thinking of switching over to corporate law because that's where the money really is."

Teddy's doctor wasn't into being funny that day. "You want to live long enough to put them through college?" he asked him bluntly. "Then you'd better get out and start exercising and begin dieting off that paunch."

Teddy groaned, but eventually gave in. The dieting was hard enough, but the exercise! It was just too much. "I can't do it," he told his brother one weekend. "I work too hard, and when I get home all I can do is flop down in front of the TV and relax."

"Yes," Joan said tartly. "And fall asleep ten minutes into Walter Cronkite . . . like a clock every night!"

"Don't worry. I've got just what you need," his brother assured him. "I'm shipping it over to you tomorrow, and my kids will set it up for you."

True to his promise, it came that Sunday and Teddy's two teen-age nephews set it up for him in the den. "It's far out," one of them said admiringly. "I'm sorry my Dad didn't stick with it. Do you like it, Uncle Teddy?"

"I'd like it better if I knew what it was," Teddy said in bewilderment, walking around the gleaming arrangement of chrome bars and wheels.

"It's a bike," his nephew explained. "You plug it in here and, hey, sit down on the seat and I'll show you. Put your feet up on the pedals and grab the handlebars." The boy turned the motorized bike on and the pedals turned as the bike's handlebars moved back and forth and the seat moved up and down.

"Hey, this is great!" Teddy said and leaned forward, grinning. "Tell your Dad I love it. I feel as if I'm zipping down the road!"

It was perfect for Teddy. He set it up in front of

the TV, and the motion of the bike kept him awake during all of Walter Cronkite. It was a bit less than perfect, however, when he went back to his family doctor for his follow-up tests.

"Your weight's all right, but I don't like the looks of this cholesterol and your HDL is too low. Did you do what I told you about exercise?"

"Did I ever! Every night for thirty minutes during the TV news." And at the doctor's puzzled frown, he explained about his motorized bike. "It's really far out."

"A little too far," the doctor said dryly. "If I wanted the bike to exercise, I'd send my bill to the bike manufacturer. Don't you see what you're doing? The bike is doing your exercise for you. You're getting nothing out of it except maybe some loosening of your muscles, and I'm not sure of that. Look, if you want to exercise in front of TV, buy a stationary bicycle."

"But that's what I've got."

"I mean one without a motor. You don't plug the bike into a socket, you plug yourself into the bike. You do your own pedaling, and there are gauges to adjust resistance. You get on that kind of bike and work up a good sweat. Half an hour a night will be perfect, as long as *you're* doing it, as long as *you* do the work yourself."

A very chastened Teddy went home to call his brother. "Send the kids over," he said sadly. "The bike has got to go."

Joan, stretched out on the floor with an exercise wheel, said, "I could have told you it wouldn't work. It was too easy. You have to do the work yourself." She grunted, from her crouched position, her hands grasping the metal dowels that projected from each side of the wheel. She pushed it forward, extending her body as far as she could, and then pulled the wheel back to its original position. Watching her curiously, Teddy asked, "What the hell is that?"

"My exercise wheel." She sat back on her heels. "It trims my waist and keeps me from getting as fat as you!"

"Very smart, but what makes you think it's better than my motorized bike?"

"Because I do the work myself, dummy." And she went back to her routine. Teddy, however, wasn't so sure, and that night he called his doctor to ask about the wheel. "Would that work for me? I could save maybe fifty bucks on a stationary bike."

"You and your gimmicks!" the doctor growled. "Look, I'm in the middle of dinner, so I'll make this short. No exercise wheel! No motorized bike! No more gimmicks! And tell Joan to stop using it. It can be a dangerous way to exercise because it could harm your lower back. Get Joan working out on that bike with you. She can watch a daytime soap opera."

In the end Teddy didn't buy the stationary bike. Instead, to save a bit, he borrowed two bikes from his oldest boys, and he and Joan began taking an hour-long ride each evening after work. Reluctantly at first, he eventually began to like it and ended up going all out for the sport. He bought bike-riding shorts, a striped racing shirt, a helmet and a very trim racing bike. "To go with my new figure," he told Joan, posing in front of the bedroom mirror. "How do you like it?"

"Very sexy. But let's get out and ride before it gets too dark."

# 11

# RUNNING AND STRETCHING

## *The Reluctant Runner*

My friend Merton is in his late forties and has gone through life at a very sedentary pace. "I let the world come to me," he told me once. "I don't exert myself—except maybe to reach for that extra portion of chocolate mousse."

Eyeing his spreading midriff, I said, "That's one exercise you can do without. Don't you ever feel impelled to get out and work off some of your excess flab?" When he shook his head complacently, I probed a bit further. "Would you be interested in a long walk through the autumn woods? A bike ride on a Saturday afternoon? A workout on the volleyball court?"

Merton shook his head and smiled. "What? Get all sweated up? Look, I'm an accountant. I work with my brain, not my hands or my body."

But a month later I ran into a sadly chastened Merton. "What's wrong?" I asked, and when he protested weakly that everything was fine, I said, "Come on. Your body language gives you away. You look like a beat pup."

"I am a beat pup," he sighed. "I've just been to see my doctor for my annual checkup and he laid down the law. The old ticker is not what is used to be and my avoirdupois has got to go!"

Merton's doctor had told him in no uncertain

terms that he must go on a rigid diet, and he had to increase his exercise. "How can I increase it," Merton protested, "when I don't exercise at all?" But the doctor insisted, and finally Merton agreed.

"So I have to exercise," Merton told me glumly. "Me, the original sedentary kid."

When Merton got home that night and told his wife what the doctor said, she nodded rather smugly. "If I've told you once, I've told you a dozen times, you need to be more active." But the question was, what kind of exercise should he go in for? That problem, Merton told me the next time we met, was solved by his married daughter. She and her husband were into jogging, and she had convinced Merton to go that route.

Now, limping along beside me, Merton sighed. "I should have stuck with my own instincts and told the doctor to bug off. My kids outfitted me with a fancy purple jogging suit, and my wife bought me a new alarm clock to get me up early enough to run before work."

"So you were off and running."

"Off and jogging, at least at first. Pretty soon I was running. I was a little surprised at myself and pleased too. I had no trouble doing two miles the first day, and every day after that I did my two miles."

"Two miles? Wow! Isn't that a lot to start with?"

"I guess I'm just in pretty good shape—or at least thought I was until the end of the month. By then I was limping like this. I had to stop running, and you know, I was right all along. A shoemaker should stick to his last. A sedentary man should stick to his chair!"

Merton went back to his doctor, and after a careful examination was told his physical shape was just fine. "You've lost weight and firmed up that flab around your middle. The jogging is good for you," he insisted. "Keep it up."

"Sure," Merton said bitterly. "My shape is fine, but my feet are killing me. You've no idea of the pain."

"You'll get used to it," the doctor said cheerfully. "I'm very pleased about your general condition. Exercise was definitely the right prescription."

"What did you do?" I asked, shaking my head sympathetically.

He shrugged. "I kept trying. I jogged for another week, but finally I had to give it up. The pain was too much. And I'm not going back to that quack. I'll just sleep an hour later each morning. Maybe the extra sleep will be as good for me as exercise!"

I had been editing a magazine for podiatrists for a number of years when I talked to Merton, and I had some idea of what his problem was. "Your doctor is right," I insisted. "Jogging *is* good for you, but if your feet are giving you trouble, the answer isn't to stop jogging. You should see a podiatrist, a foot doctor."

Over Merton's protests, I took him to visit a podiatrist I had worked with on my magazine. While the doctor examined his feet, Merton said, "I guess I have weak feet and just can't jog or run." There was a hopeful note in his voice.

"You're almost fifty," the foot doctor answered. "You've worked at a desk all your life and it isn't easy to start jogging after all those sedentary years."

"Then I shouldn't jog?" Merton asked with a sigh

of relief.

"Of course you should jog!" the doctor snapped. "According to your internist, it's helping your general health."

"First you tell me I shouldn't jog," Merton said with annoyance, "then you tell me I should. Please make up your mind."

"I said at your age you shouldn't start jogging all at once."

"I can't get any younger."

"But you can get smarter. Now seriously, what you have to do first is to give those feet a rest. No jogging for at least two weeks, maybe three if they're still sore. You're lucky that there's nothing basically wrong with your feet. It's just that you've made the two most common mistakes of all new runners and joggers, and believe me, with this new craze for running I see a lot of this."

"What two mistakes?"

"The first mistake is starting off by running the full distance the first time. Start small. Jog before you run, and then do a quarter of a mile each day for the first week. No more."

"How do I measure a quarter of a mile?" Merton asked.

The doctor looked Merton up and down. "You're about six feet tall. Your average pace should be, let's see, about three feet, that's around a thousand seven hundred and sixty paces to a mile. Jog four hundred and forty paces each day. When you feel up to it, add another quarter mile. Build up in small increments and let your feet get accustomed to jogging. After all, you can't let a machine go virtually unused for years and still expect it to function perfectly."

"And building up slowly will take care of the

171

pain in my feet?"

"It will help correct the most common mistake, starting off with a bang. The second mistake is where you run. What kind of surface do you run on?"

Merton shrugged. "The sidewalk."

"Hard concrete?"

"Most of it, except where it needs repair."

"You know, you might as well hit the soles of your feet with a hammer. Each running or jogging step on concrete is traumatic. Walking on concrete is hard enough on the feet. But running? No. If you're young, it might be okay, but at your age, stay away from cement. Find a cinder track if you can, maybe at your local high school or a dirt path in the park, but not cement, not at forty!"

Merton nodded. "I'm beginning to see the light."

"Now, a third error, not so common these days. What do you jog in?"

"My kids bought me a jogging suit . . . "

"No, no." The doctor frowned. "I mean on your feet. What do you wear on your feet when you jog?"

"Tennis shoes."

"Well, tennis shoes wouldn't be too bad if you built up slowly and jogged on cinders. You need something soft between your feet and the path. Even better than tennis shoes, get yourself fitted with a good pair of running shoes. They're available all over. Be sure they fit well. They'll cushion your feet against whatever you run on, but I'd still stay clear of hard surfaces. Now if your feet still hurt after all that, come back and see me again. I won't charge you for the visit."

Merton never needed the free visit. The simple three-part program did the trick. (1) Begin jogging or running slowly and build up. (Now the same is true for any exercise.) (2) Jog or run on a cinder track, dirt or grass or even hard sand if you possibly can. (3) Wear a good pair of running shoes that fit well.

"What I don't understand," Merton told me a few months later when we were both out jogging around the local high-school track, "is how so many people get away with running on cement. I see it all over, and it doesn't seem to bother the runners."

"If they start out with a good pair of running shoes, they can usually get away with it," I said. "Especially if they're young and have built up gradually. But at our age, it's courting disaster."

In jogging, the danger to the feet, and the heart too for that matter, usually comes about because someone like Merton, who had done very little physical exercise all his life, suddenly starts running or jogging with no build-up. The body usually cannot take this sudden strain after decades of inaction. Merton was lucky. Many men his age, plunging into a heavy program of exercise, suddenly end up with a heart attack. Merton not only avoided this problem, he got "into" running; he took it on wholeheartedly. He built up his distance slowly, as the doctor had advised him, but as the weeks passed it became two miles a day, then three, four, five and six.

"I don't think it's good at your age," his wife

fretted, but Merton brushed her protests aside. "I feel like a million bucks. In fact, it wouldn't hurt you one bit to get out with me some mornings and start jogging too."

"Me?" His wife looked alarmed. "I have enough to do around the house in the morning without getting into that routine."

"Pity," Merton said thoughtfully. "Irma says it saved her life—running, that is."

"And who's Irma?" his wife asked suspiciously.

"One of the women I run with. She says that after her divorce everything seemed to fall apart. She was just miserable. She told me she almost overdosed on sleeping pills once, and then she discovered running. It's really been her salvation. It straightened out her head, and now she's thinking of the Boston Marathon—a great gal."

"You've really gotten to know her," his wife said slowly. She was silent after that, but the next week Merton brought up Irma again. "She thinks I should start training for the Boston Marathon. She says I have an incredible stride. You know, I think I could do it. Irma says all I need is confidence."

"I think," his wife said carefully, "I might just start jogging with you in the morning. I've noticed I feel sort of sluggish during the day."

Merton became more and more enthusiastic about the marathon and began to stretch his distance out, then abruptly all his plans ended in disaster. He was up to ten miles when he decided one weekend to try for twelve. "If you can do twelve," he told his wife as they jogged out to the track, "you should be able to do twenty-six—that's the rule of thumb they use for the race."

But at the eight-mile mark, Merton doubled over in pain. His wife was barely able to get him home. His right calf muscle was knotted up and he couldn't put any weight on that foot. Rest brought some relief but not much, and by phone the doctor advised him to try wet heat and then, somehow, limp over to his office. "It doesn't sound too serious. I'd come and see you, but I don't make house calls on principle."

When Merton arrived at the office, the doctor shook his head. "You've got a bad case of Achilles tendonitis. Your Achilles tendon is right behind your heel, here, feel it. It's inflamed. I'll give you some medication and you keep off it for a while."

"But what about the marathon?" Merton asked.

"You're out of your mind! I want you to cut back on this running," the doctor said firmly. "Enough is too much. You take it easy now. Two miles a day is fine. Forget the marathon."

### The Big Stretch

But back home, a visit from Irma gave Merton hope. "I had the same thing last year," she told him and his wife, "and I helped cure it with stretching. That's why I stretch before and after I run. You see, running knots up your muscles. Stretching eases them out."

Irma was right. The tendency to plunge into running or almost any exercise without a careful program of stretching can do a great deal of damage to the muscles. Just what is stretching? Well, hang around any running area, the school track or a path in the park, and you'll see most of the runners going through some weird contortions before and after they run. They'll stretch out their legs on a park rail, or stand leaning into the trunk of a tree from four feet away, or they'll bend to touch their toes and hold the bend for what seems an interminable time. They're all doing stretching exercises.

Stretching is becoming almost as popular as running is this season and tennis was last, but it's more than a passing fad. Done before and after a sport or a workout, it will keep your muscles flexible and prevent injuries such as the Achilles tendonitis that Merton came down with, or shin splints, a painful condition of the lower leg, or any one of a dozen muscle problems. It's a good safeguard against tennis elbow, and football coaches are making it compulsory for the teams before and after playing.

Stretching can be of tremendous benefit, or it can harm the would-be athlete if it's done incorrectly. Instead of stretching only for muscle flexibility, the perfect stretch will also reduce muscle tension and get freer movement in the body. In addition, there is a calming effect when stretching is well done. It relaxes you and soothes your mind while it helps you get into the mental mood for exercise. It also helps calm you down afterwards.

In many ways, stretching goes beyond athletics and exercise. It can relieve the tightness a secretary or business executive feels after sitting all day at a desk. It can limber you up during and after a long car ride, or it can take a good deal of the ache out of housework.

There's no set time for stretching. You should do it before and after exercise, certainly, but you can also do it when you wake up or when you're watching television or even while you're sitting and reading. The greatest thing about stretching is the simple fact that, done properly, it feels good!

Stretching should be done without strain or pain.

It does no good to stretch a muscle till it hurts. In fact it can do some harm. The muscle will react to the pain by knotting up into a cramp. Go to the point of mild tension. The tension will ease off by the end of a twenty-second stretch.

Once you've mastered this technique of reaching the point of tension, go a bit beyond it to that delicate point where it almost hurts but not quite. Never go beyond this.

If you build up slowly, the "almost hurt" will ease off, and you'll know that the muscle had been properly stretched. Never bounce into a stretch. It pulls the muscle out too abruptly and can be dangerous. Instead, ease into it as far as your body will comfortably take you.

The stretching exercise that helped Merton with his tendonitis would also have prevented the condition from developing if he had done thirty seconds of it before and after each run. A combination of five minutes of this and other stretching exercises will keep any runner in cramp-free condition. The stretch that helps Achilles tendonitis can be done against a tree or wall, with one foot about four feet from the wall, the other foot close. The back leg is the one that will be stretched, and after half a minute, the legs' positions should be changed. Straightening the back leg out while you bend the other knee will allow you to feel the stretch in your calf muscle, the muscle that pulls the Achilles tendon.

Another stretch that helps prepare you for almost any exercise can be done by sitting on the ground and placing the soles of your feet together, then pulling them towards your body as far as they will comfortably go. Let your knees flop apart, and you'll feel the stretch in your groin muscles.

Stretching can be done by many different

methods, and there's a stretch for almost every muscle in the body. I have seen runners stretch their Achilles tendons while waiting at a cross street for the light to turn. They turn their backs to the traffic, place their toes on the curb and let their heels drop towards street level. The front of the foot is bent up by the weight of the body on the heels, and the tendon is stretched.

There are many books that give good picture guides to stretching, and perhaps the best of them was written by Bob Anderson who has taught stretching to the Denver Broncos, the New York Jets and the Los Angeles Dodgers among other teams. His book is called, very simply, *Stretching,* and it contains a series of stretches for almost all of the common sports.

The advice Bob Anderson gives, again and again, is to work within your limits. "You may think that if you work within your limits there will be little or no improvement," he says. "On the contrary, as you learn your present limits, you also learn that it is possible to increase those limits gradually over a period of time."

My friend Merton learned this the hard way, but he did eventually learn it. A program of stretching cured his Achilles tendonitis, and a regular stretching before and after each run enabled him slowly to increase his distance without trouble. The last I heard, he had entered the New York Marathon.

"At least it's better than the Boston Marathon. It has no heartbreak hill," he told me. "And I'm sure I can make the distance—maybe in five or six hours, but I'll make it!"

And Irma? "The last I heard, she had run off with an Australian who finished among the first ten in the Boston Marathon."

# 12

# SECRET, DIFFERENT AND UNUSUAL

## Breaking the Vicious Circle

One of my favorite rendezvous is with an old, old friend—old on two counts. I've known Grace for over forty years, and Grace is old. "On the wrong side of eighty," as she puts it. I hadn't seen Grace in over a year, and now as we sat in her pleasant living room one rainy afternoon sipping tea, I was surprised at how slim and erect she was, and more surprised at the easy way she moved. I told her so, and she laughed. "So you remember my arthritis."

I nodded. "But last year you were in such pain."

Smiling, she pushed back her short, white hair. "And that was when you chose to scold me about getting no exercise. I didn't even get out and walk, I hurt so much. The dreadful thing about arthritis is that we can't exercise because it's so painful, and unless we exercise we get stiffer and stiffer and even more painful. I call it a vicious circle—but I've broken out of it!"

"You mean you exercise now?" I was delighted. "But how?"

She leaned back, cradling her teacup in her hands. "The cup's heat feels so good to my joints, especially on a day like this. Now bad weather is deadly to me. You know, after I talked to you last year, I tried a health club."

"To work out in the gym?" I was shocked.

She shivered. "With my joints? Never! I joined to swim, and the swimming was fine. It was the only exercise I've been able to do for years. I built up to six laps, and I felt marvelous. You know, the water takes the weight off my joints." She leaned back with a little frown. "Trouble was, it was such an effort to get to the club, especially in weather like this. And it was expensive. I live on a pretty tight budget, and the health-club rates kept going up. Then too, on bad days like this I'd have to take a cab, and you know what that costs. I'd get tense about going and I'd begin to wonder if the good results were worth the tension involved. Arthritis is affected by tension, you know."

"Indeed I do. But you seem to have licked the problem. How did you do it?"

"To be truthful, I didn't. My niece, Melissa did. She's a physiotherapist, and at her last visit she read me a lecture, just as you did, about exercise. When I told her how difficult it was to get out, she said, 'I'm going to give you a set of exercises that you can do right here in your living room, and they won't hurt your arthritis.' And the little darling did just that."

I was intrigued. "Did they work?"

"Well, look at me!" She put down her teacup, and standing up, bent down to touch the floor, then straightened up very smoothly. "Pretty classy for an eighty-year-old lady, eh? And no pain."

"Well, don't keep me in suspense. Show me the exercises."

"Well, they're so gentle you don't really think of them as exercises. You feel no pulling or stretching, and best of all, no pain. After a while your muscles loosen up and your joints become freer. You see, with rheumatoid arthritis like mine the joints become so painful you get afraid to move. The lack of movement aggravates the condition—the same old vicious circle.''

"And these exercises? How do they work?''

"Well, I'll show you. The first one you do sitting in a regular chair.'' Grace sat down in a stiff-backed Victorian chair, held her head erect, then dropped it to her chest and lifted it. "See, that's all there is to it. I do that five times, like all the exercises.''

"That's all? Just bending your head and lifting it? What kind of an exercise is that?''

"A very, very gentle one. In the second exercise I drop my head to the left, straighten up, then drop it to the right, like this. Then I turn to the left, try to touch my shoulder with my chin, then to the right to repeat it. Each motion five times and I'm finished with the head. Simple?''

"Simple and beautiful, if it works.''

"Oh, it does. All the joints in my neck are moved, without pain.''

Grace went on to show me the rest of the exercises. To exercise her trunk, she held her arms out and twisted to each side, then bent to each side. She lifted her arms, breathed in as she did, then dropped them, breathing out.

The legs were simple. Still sitting, she straightened each leg in turn, then lifting her feet from the floor, she turned them in and out to move the ankle joints.

That was the sitting part. Very spritely, Grace stretched out on her back on the rug with her arms at her sides. The motion here was to raise the arms over her head, then lower them. Then, her arms on the rug, her palms up, she moved her arms in big

181

swings from above her head to her sides. "It makes me feel as if I'm flying," she laughed. "We used to do this in the snow when we were kids, and we called it making butterflies. Do kids still do it?"

She clasped her hands behind her head and brought her elbows together, then apart. "For that matter," she said, "What do kids do now to play?" She held her arms at her sides, then brought her hands to her shoulders and straightened them. Then she moved her forearms from her sides to her stomach.

"I can see you've exercised your shoulders and elbows."

"Right, and now the wrists." With elbows bent, she turned her palms towards her face, then out, then made a fist, straightened the fingers, separated them and wiggled them. All the joints in her hand had been moved.

The spinal column came next. She stretched her arms forward till her head and shoulders were pulled off the rug, then she lifted each knee and brought it up to her chest. To move her hips, she stretched each leg to the side. "Only as far as it will go comfortably," she cautioned. "That's important Melissa told me. Movement without strain." With her arms flat on the rug she pulled her feet forward towards her face, then away. That did the ankle joints.

Grace's last exercise was to roll onto her stomach and like a rocking horse, first raise her head and shoulders, then each leg from the thigh, bending her knees. When she finally got to her feet, grinning at my surprise, she said. "And that's the second time I've done them today. I usually do these the first thing in the morning when I wake up. It gets me over the stiffness of the night." She peered at the tea tray. "I think I'll reward myself with an extra piece of that nice raisin cake you brought."

"Those exercises may loosen you up," I said, "but they won't take off weight. You know that."

She grinned. "Who cares about weight. The men stopped whistling long ago. But I still manage to keep my figure. I really eat very little."

What impressed me about Grace's exercises was that every joint in her body was moved, without strain and without putting any weight on it. "I don't go beyond five times for each one," she told me. "Melissa told me that too much would bring on the pain of that vicious circle, and I'd lose more than the mobility I gain. But that's the real joy of all this, mobility. I can get around without pain." She looked at the window and sighed. "Except of course on a rainy day like this. How about some more cake?"

I said, "I'll take a piece for the rain."

The thing I liked about Grace's exercises was the ease with which they were done. There was no strain, no discomfort. They were, in a way, very much like the stretching exercises my friend Merton finally learned. But stretching is usually done to counteract muscle tightness. This was the first time I had seen a variation of it done to mobilize joints and keep them mobile.

## A Hidden Pleasure

There was a private quality to Grace's exercise and it reminded me of my friend Lazlo and his secret for staying trim. I met Lazlo when we both worked for a large drug company in Philadelphia. There was a quiet elegance to Lazlo. His body was very slim and erect, and he dressed well. He favored dark-blue suits and light-blue shirts with royal blue ties. When I asked him once why he wore nothing else, he confessed that he was unsure of colors. "My sister once told me I looked good in this outfit," he said, gesturing at his clothes, "so when I went to work here I bought five blue suits and ten blue shirts, all the same. Oh yes, I have six blue ties. I never have any trouble matching things up."

At first I thought he was putting me on, but as we got to know each other better, I realized that he was serious about his clothes. That was really the way he dressed. One week we were on a business trip together, a very grueling trip, and I was amazed at Lazlo's stamina. "How the hell do you do it?" I asked. "You really have a fantastic endurance."

"Exercise," he shrugged. "That's the big secret."

But there was something a little evasive about his answer, and that evening when we were having a drink in the bar of our hotel, I pressed him for an explanation. "Do you belong to a gym, Lazlo?"

"Oh, no."

"Tennis?" He laughed and shook his head, and I pushed on. "Are you a runner? A cyclist? Soccer?" I went down the list of all the sports I knew as Lazlo kept chuckling.

Finally he said, "I'll give you one hint. I enjoy my exercise out of all proportion to the good it does."

That fascinated me. "Now you've got to explain."

He turned his glass on the bar. "Usually, when you do something that's good for you, like exercise, it gets to be a chore. I've tried jogging and all those other good-for-you sports, and I didn't like any of them. I knew something was wrong. All the exercises I tried were a drag. The trouble was, I hated the flab I was putting on without exercise. I'm pretty vain about the way I look, and I knew I had to find some sort of routine I could stay with. Another thing driving me was that when I did get to exercise, I felt great, physically, not mentally. It seemed a tough choice—feel great but be bored. No boredom, and be a slob."

"But you did finally find something you like?"

Lazlo had a funny look on his face and sipped his drink slowly. "You've boxed me into a corner. I do have a secret exercise that keeps me in shape and feeling good. The thing is, I've never confessed it to anyone."

"But you'll tell me, won't you?" I signaled the bartender for another drink.

"The truth is . . . " he paused, looked at me, then looked down. "I've been a frustrated ballet dancer all my life."

"Ballet?" I was truly surprised. "No kidding?"

"Oh, I never had any formal training. To tell you the truth, I've never had any training at all. I'm too self-conscious to take lessons, and in the town where I grew up, well—ballet lessons would have been a direct slight on my manhood. But I've read every book on ballet I could get my hands on, and I learned the warm-up and basic steps from the books. I practice every morning—only, I don't call it practice." Frowning, he went on slowly. "I don't know how to explain this. Maybe it's just my personal fantasy, but once I put on a record and

185

begin to dance around the apartment, I'm on a stage and I can hear the audience, even see the footlights and spots, and I completely forget myself in the spell of the dance.''

Fascinated, I asked, "Are you good at it? Would you really like to be a professional someday?"

Lazlo made an impatient gesture. "I don't want that. I'm not that good, and I started too late. I'm not really stagestruck. This is something I do because it gives me pleasure and keeps my body in shape, and you know something? Ballet is one of the most grueling exercises there is. I'm sweating and panting like a truck horse after thirty minutes.''

"And you really wouldn't want it to be your life's work?"

"No way! Look, in my own private fantasy I can be as good as I want. I can outdance Baryshnikov. Who's to compare us?" He laughed. "Over and above the fantasy and the fun, there is the pure pleasure I get out of dancing. Sometimes I go beyond my usual time. On a Saturday or Sunday I'll work out for an hour. It's something I can look forward to, the carrot on the stick that gets me through the dull business day. I look forward to my time alone with my dance music.''

"There's one thing that puzzles me," I said. "Why didn't you ever go in for it as a career, when you were young, I mean."

"That was my father's doing," Lazlo said flatly. "He caught me playing at ballet dancing when I was just a kid. I had been to see *The Nutcracker* with my mother—that was out in Omaha when I was just a kid, and the whole thing made a tremendous impression on me. My father was furious. He told me straight out that ballet dancers weren't real men, and I was to forget about it. He wasn't to catch me doing it again—and he didn't. I became a closet balletomaniac and read everything I could about it till I left home and came East. Then I could see as much as I wanted, but it was too late to do anything about my own dancing, or at least I thought it was. One summer I became very friendly with a professional ballet dancer and I was impressed with his dedication. You know, he practiced hours every day. When I confessed my longing, he asked why didn't I do something about it. I told him I was too old, but he said not professionally, just for my own fun. He helped me with some of the basics and I was off."

Curiously I asked, "Was that ballet dancer what your father thought?"

Lazlo shrugged. "I don't know, or care for that matter. He was a good dancer. The point is, I know what I am, and that's what matters. As far as ballet being a manly art, have you any idea of the energy it takes to dance professionally, of the strength and endurance? I'd match a ballet dancer against a football player any day." He laughed. "The only thing I miss is the beautiful ballerina to lift."

I raised my glass. "I'll keep my eyes open for one."

"Do that. It would be the icing on the cake!"


### The Inefficient Housewife

Years later I told a woman friend of mine about Lazlo, and she shrugged. "I think the private part is fun, keeping something like that all to yourself, but as for it being unusual—I've been dancing for

187

exercise for years."

"I'd like to know more about that."

"Why not. Mine isn't private at all. As a matter of fact, I get together with a group of my friends, and we dance our little hearts out."

"I gather it's aerobic dancing."

She shook her head. "No, although I guess it achieves the same thing. We're just not that structured about it. Oh, we have our warm-up, a few stretches the way runners have, and we cool down afterwards with more stretching, but the point is, we just dance. Mostly it's to a disco beat, and it's energetic, believe me. We go at it hot and heavy for about twenty minutes to a half hour, and we get our pulse rate up too. It's exercise, but it's fun. All of us love to dance, and it just happens that we all have husbands or lovers who couldn't care less about it, dancing, I mean. So this gives us a chance to get it out of our systems and to keep in trim. It's good for our heart, and it's good for our shape."

She was quite right. Twenty minutes to a half hour of dancing, especially strenuous disco dancing, gets the pulse rate up about as high as running. Done at least three times a week, it's a grand exercise, and for a lot of people, men as well as women, a pleasurable one.

What my friend liked about it was this pleasurable quality. They danced in each other's homes, and there were no expenses involved. I was reminded of that lack of expense when I had lunch at the home of a close friend recently. I hadn't seen Babs since the birth of her second baby, and I was delighted to find her full of vitality and fun, with none of the worn-out quality of new mothers. Best of all she had lost all the extra weight she put on with her pregnancy.

I watched her clear the table, one dish at a time, then bring in the dessert, again one dish at a time, and I realized that she had been doing this all during the meal. "What you could use," I told her as she sat down, "is a good time-and-motion man. I've never seen so much wasted movement!"

Babs laughed. "You don't understand that I'm doing it all deliberately. I make four trips to do what should take me only two trips, even one. It's the same when I clean up. I use the maximum amount of effort. I make a dozen trips to the kitchen and to my cleaning cupboard. I walk around the bed four times when I make it. I use two or three times the effort I need on everything."

"For heaven's sake, why?" I was shocked. "Why be so inefficient? I could organize this place for you in half an hour."

"Don't you dare!" She laughed. "True efficiency depends on how you look at it. I'm being a very inefficient housewife, but a very efficient exerciser."

"Aha!" A light was dawning. "You mean . . ."

"Exactly. I'm tied down to a house these days, and I've accepted that. I'm really and truly a housewife, and you know, I like it. The children are darling, and I've set up the attic as a studio and I get to do some painting up there when they nap, or when I don't have a guest like you to lunch."

"Tell me more about this housework-exercise."

"Sure. Have some more bread. I baked it myself."

"With how many extra trips to the oven? It's good."

"You ought to see my arms from all the kneading. I've done away with shortcuts and efficiency around the house. I've given up working since I had the kids, but I don't want to put on all that housewifely flab. I diet, but I need something to keep my body toned up and my muscles working. So whenever I can, I move. I double and triple the number of trips I make around the house. I sit down and jump up a dozen times during a meal. When I'm changing the baby or cleaning, I bend and stretch and go about it as vigorously as I can.

"I never ask Tom to get me things from the next room. I go myself. He thinks I'm a devoted wife, but the truth is I'm selfish. If I were all that devoted I'd make him move his butt too. As it is, I do it all for the extra movement I get out of it."

I had to laugh. "Are you this inefficient outside of the house, too?"

"Of course," Babs grinned. "When I take a bus anywhere I get off two or three stops before mine and walk the extra distance—if I take a bus at all. Any distance under two miles I walk. And stairs—I run up them whenever I get a chance. It's something I think of as . . . well, I feel I'm fooling everyone else."

"I don't get that."

"I don't consider any of this work. I think of it as exercise, something for my own good, a sort of game, you see, because I'm the one who's gaining by it all. It's fun, because I treat it that way."

"Is it always fun?"

"Well, of course it isn't always fun. There are times when I'm bushed and it's hard going on, but there are times when any game is hard, or any exercise. What could be harder than finishing a marathon? No, it's all in the way you look at it. I've turned housework and being a mother into an exercise routine." She put her hands on her hips and turned around. "And it's paid off. I look great and I know it."

I had to agree. "You do indeed."

I think that the most pleasure Babs got out of her housewife routine was the fact that no one—not even her husband—realized what she was up to. Most of her friends were going through the housewife and mother routine, and all of them envied the way she managed to stay so slim and healthy. The funny thing about it all was that doing as much work as her friends, indeed more—for she did it with deliberate inefficiency—left her much less tired than they were. "I've decided it's not the work that tires a housewife," she told me, "it's the monotony and boredom and the distaste for what you're doing. I've avoided that."


## The Wiggle Walkers

For those who can't run or jog but would still like to get out at the crack of dawn and get their daily exercise in before breakfast, "racewalking" may be the answer. Getting started that early doesn't interfere with the day's routine, and it leaves you feeling mellow and yet alert enough to tackle the day.

A growing amount of orthopedic evidence claims that among runners and joggers there is an increasing incidence of Achilles tendonitis, shin splints, runner's knee and low back pains. Not everyone who runs will develop these, but there are some who will. It doesn't mean that running is bad for you, but it does mean that these people need an alternate exercise. Mickey was one of these, and "racewalking" was his alternative.

"For my part," Mickey complained to me, "running or jogging is out. I can't take the pounding. My joints ache and my feet aren't all that good. After only half a mile I feel as if I've been through a washing machine. Walking? No problems. Running? Forget it!"

Mickey was a perfect candidate for racewalking, but when we discussed it he was doubtful about it. "You mean, become one of those guys who wiggle their hips when they walk? Hey, come on!"

Mickey had a strong dose of "macho," and the racewalking image bothered him. He was a little less bothered when he discovered that racewalking is one of the sports at the Olympic Games. More of his uneasiness disappeared the first time he saw a group of pro racewalkers and then tried it out himself. He suddenly understood that need for the hip wiggle.

According to the International Amateur Athletic Federation, racewalking as a sport is very carefully defined as "a progression of steps so taken that unbroken contact with the ground is maintained." In running or jogging, by contrast, there are times when both feet are off the ground at once. The impact of the entire body hitting down on that one foot as it makes contact again can cause injury. In short runs of two or three miles, the injuries seldom occur, but in long runs they are very common. Dr. George Sheehan, who has written extensively on running and is himself an accomplished runner, has noted that any runner who averages fifty miles a week "has a seventy-three percent chance of suffering an injury that will sideline him for a considerable length of time."

The Federation, describing racewalking, goes on

to note that "at each step the advancing foot of the walker must make contact with the ground before the rear foot leaves the ground." This overcomes the problem of the pounding shock a runner endures. Describing the stride, the Federation says, "The leg must be straightened at least for one moment, and in particular, the supportive leg must be straightened in the vertical upright position."

Mickey, once he got into the technique of race-walking, found it had one advantage over running or jogging. "It develops the arms and chest as well as the legs," he told me. "You hold them high and pump them back and forth to develop speed. After a few months I found my entire upper body was developing."

Another positive aspect of racewalking is the way the foot is placed. Howard Jacobson, president of the New York Walkers Club and a former Olympic coach, suggests that by placing the feet straight with each step, both the front and back musculature of the leg are strengthened. In running, however, only the calf muscles are strengthened.

A third advantage is the very "wiggle" that Mickey shuddered at. To increase his stride, the racewalker throws his hip forward, and this forward wiggle adds extra pull to strengthen the leg muscles.

"The big thing about racewalking," Mickey confided to me recently, "is that there's no real age differential. It's not a young person's sport, nor an old one's. I walk with a sixty-year-old woman and an eighteen-year-old man, and the sixty-year-old can easily keep up with both of us."

Watching Mickey in one of his recent races, I thought I recognized one of the other contestants. I went up to him afterwards and asked if we knew each other. "I've seen you someplace, I'm sure," I said.

"Do you run?" When I nodded, he said, "Around the reservoir?" I nodded again, and he shrugged. "Well, that's it. I run there every morning."

I said, "Of course, but if you're a runner, what are you doing here?"

"Hey, a lot of us are runners. Racewalking doesn't cancel out running. In fact, if anything, it helps. It teaches me how to keep from injuring myself by showing me how to place my foot properly when I come down on it, and it actually helps me increase my time. You know, I started racewalking when I injured my foot running. It's a funny thing, but you can racewalk through an injury which would keep you from running. I had a bad Achilles tendon injury, and I had to stop running. I was able to racewalk, though, and it actually helped the tendon heal without stiffening up."

Confirmation of his contention that a runner and a racewalker could switch sports came in 1979 when Howard Jacobson, an accomplished race-walker, finished in the middle of a field of 10,000 runners in the New York Marathon's 26-mile run.

# 13

## CONVERSATION WITH A PHYSIOTHERAPIST

Sweating it out . . . pounding the flesh . . . race-walking—a dizzying array of alternatives. But what kinds of exercise are right for different kinds of people? How do you know what exercise is best for you? To get some answers, I spoke to Beverly Devine, Unit Supervisor of Physical Therapy at the Institute for Rehabilitative Medicine in New York City.

*Fast:* Is there an age at which we should stop exercising?

*Devine:* I don't believe there is.

*Fast:* Can you go right up through your eighties and nineties and still continue to exercise?

*Devine:* That depends on what kind of exercise you're talking about.

*Fast:* Can you give me an example of the kind of exercise that someone past sixty should be doing?

*Devine:* I can, only if I know what they have been doing up to the age of sixty. It also has to do with the type of life they have led. In general I would say that walking is the safest type of exercise for anyone over sixty.

*Fast:* Well let's take your average man or woman who has led a sedentary life until sixty and then decides, after being exposed to all the propaganda about exercise that is currently being thrown around, to go out and get into the active swing of things. Is there a sensible program for someone like that?

*Devine:* Yes. There is always some kind of program that can be developed, but I must repeat: It depends on the individual. A person should see a doctor first to find out if exercise is really the right thing. Then, and this is important, any exercise program he or she chooses should start gradually and build up slowly. The danger comes when someone who has been sedentary all his life decides to exercise and goes "gung ho" into the full routine. That's very bad for the body. I want to stress those two points. One, get medical clearance before you start exercising and two, build up gradually. Start with a moderate amount and increase it slowly over a sensible period of time.

*Fast:* Okay. Let's say our exerciser starts with walking. Where does he go from there?

*Devine:* He can gradually increase the intensity, walk faster, get into brisk walking, or he can increase his distance or go for a longer walk. That may well be sufficient for someone like that. He wouldn't need a more complex routine.

There are also some general stretching exercises that the older person can do to stay limber. There are also breathing exercises that will help the respiratory capability.

*Fast:* What sort of exercises would be good to increase respiratory capability?

*Devine:* Just breathing properly and fully while doing some general mobility exercises—stretching, bending, reaching.

*Fast:* What if this sedentary person of sixty-plus wants to push farther and go into, let's say, a program of jogging. Can he do this if his doctor gives him the okay?

*Devine:* Why not? Providing he builds up very gradually.

*Fast:* What if jogging or walking is a bore? What else can you recommend?

*Devine:* As I said, there are general mobility programs for older people, programs that take their age into account. They're similar to toned-down calisthenics.

*Fast:* What if they want something more strenuous?

*Devine:* Let me emphasize again the gradual buildup and a medical exam first.

*Fast:* Yes, but if all that is done, suppose they still want to be more active? What other choices are there besides walking and jogging?

*Devine:* Running and bicycling. Cycling, if it is done sensibly, is good for the legs and respiration. Even a stationary bike is good. Swimming is excellent.

*Fast:* What about tennis or racquetball?

*Devine:* They are both rather strenuous for someone just starting.

*Fast:* But once they've built up to it, is it a good idea to go into a sport like either of those? Or are they both potentially dangerous? Is there any condition in older people that should make them leery of such strenuous exercise?

*Devine:* Well, tennis and racquetball are both vigorous games. My father is near seventy and not athletic. If he wanted to get into a game type of exercise, I'd take him out on the tennis court and let him lob a few balls around, but I wouldn't let him run around the court!

*Fast:* Why not?

*Devine:* At that age there's a calcium loss in bones. They are more brittle, and also people are not as quick-moving as they once were. Their coordination may not be all that good.

*Fast:* Is that true for both men and women?

*Devine:* Yes.

*Fast:* But let's say our sixty-plus man has been athletic all his life and functions at the "training level." Would you have him slow down?

*Devine:* No.

*Fast:* What would you warn him against?

*Devine:* I would only be worried about his endurance. Of course, if he's in shape and has exercised all his life, it's a different story.

*Fast:* Let's consider the group of people whose age ranges from thirty to sixty, a group not active before. Do the same rules apply? Should these younger people have a medical checkup first?

*Devine:* It's not as necessary, of course, but if they're going into exercise very seriously, then yes, I think they should.

*Fast:* At what age should a person consider a medical checkup before starting an exercise program? At thirty or forty or fifty?

*Devine:* If the person is obese and hasn't exercised in years, I'd say check it out with a doctor at any age.

*Fast:* But what about someone who's not obese, who's maybe only ten, fifteen, or twenty pounds overweight. Should someone like that get a medical checkup, too?

*Devine:* If he hasn't exercised before, I feel that the safest thing is to get a checkup. The point is, you want to make sure your cardiac condition is okay.

*Fast:* You're really saying a medical checkup is good at any age.

*Devine:* Except for children.

*Fast:* When does childhood end?

*Devine:* I'd say at twenty, unless you know something is wrong. If a child has, say a heart murmur, then a medical exam is indicated.

*Fast:* Let's take a look at the sedentary thirties and forties. Is there one particular exercise better than the others for someone in that age range? Let's say we're discussing someone who has no inclination towards exercise of any kind. He simply feels, I've got to do something. What should he do?

*Devine:* When I'm dealing with someone like that, I try to explore a program he'd enjoy, because exercisers *must* enjoy what they're doing. They shouldn't do it just because it's good for them or because they feel guilty if they don't.

*Fast:* Are there any questions you can ask yourself to find out if a particular exercise is best for you?

*Devine:* Yes. You ask yourself first, do I want a regular routine of exercise alone at a regular time of day? Then, would I like to exercise in the company of others? Do I like competitive exercise? Do I prefer exercise indoors or out?

The point is, you see, the exercise should be geared to your own likes and dislikes.

*Fast:* Are there any danger signs to watch for, any cautions you might suggest?

*Devine:* Oh, yes. Watch out for any unusual body reactions to exercise—pains in the chest, shortness of breath that lasts a few days, pain in the joints.

*Fast:* And if the would-be exerciser still feels it's a drag?

*Devine:* I would suggest more social activity tied to

exercise, group exercise, games.

*Fast:* Can exercise pose any problems to women? For instance, can it harm their breasts?

*Devine:* The general feeling is that as long as they wear a good bra it can't do any harm. However, large-breasted women may feel some discomfort and decide not to continue their exercise because of it.

*Fast:* Are there any problems women face that are different from men's problems?

*Devine:* This is a controversial area, but my own opinion is that there is a problem if the exercise is taken to extreme degrees. For example, body-contact sports should be avoided. But women can compete well in most sports, although we have tended to overprotect them.

*Fast:* Are there any programs particularly good for people in their twenties and thirties?

*Devine:* Walking, jogging, cycling and swimming are all good. So are dancing, skipping rope, running in place, racquetball, soccer, basketball— any of these, as long as it's a continuous exercise. I'm partial to the Air Force exercises and to aerobic exercises, aerobic dancing if you like to dance. There are many different aerobic dance programs in which people get together for ballet, disco or other kinds of dancing. I want to stress again the importance of the exerciser being interested in whatever program he selects. It shouldn't be a chore.

*Fast:* What qualifications should an exercise have to make it a good one?

*Devine:* The exercise program should be long enough.

*Fast:* How long is enough?

*Devine:* That depends on how intense the exercise is. The more intense, the shorter the duration. The less intense, the longer it should take. As a guide, I'd say, once you've built yourself up, the minimum should be fifteen to thirty minutes of hard exercise, say three or four times a week.

*Fast:* That is in terms of cardiac respiratory fitness. What about exercise for weight loss?

*Devine:* You have to decide first how much you want to lose. Roughly, if you are overweight by ten pounds, you need to burn up a hundred extra calories a day. For every hundred calories, you need about ten minutes of hard exercise. You can figure up or down from that. Of course, you must add to all of this the warm-up and cool-down periods. About five or ten minutes are needed for each. Stretching and bending exercises are best.

Exercise should be geared to the particular problem you are trying to manage. Do you want to increase circulo-respiratory endurance? Then slant the program towards increased endurance, not so strenuous but a longer period of time—walking or racewalking for example. If the problem is weight reduction, any exercise that involves large muscle masses is good, especially if it is continued for a long time.

I would also go for mobility exercises—stretching, bending, reaching—especially of those areas where fat is concentrated.

*Fast:* I can't believe you mean spot-reducing!

*Devine:* No. We both know that's not possible, but you can tighten your muscles in certain areas. You can't redistribute fat, but you can change the body proportions by changing the muscular aspect of the body, and you can do that through calisthenics and modified weightlifting as well as isometric and isotonic exercises.

*Fast:* What if you are exercising just to feel better?

*Devine:* Then I would advise outdoor exercises and competitive sports.

# 14

## CONVERSATION WITH
## A CARDIOLOGIST

Beverly Devine, the physiotherapist, feels that the best exercise program, once you've consulted with a physician and built yourself up, should involve fifteen to thirty minutes of hard exercise, at least three or four times a week. To learn more about "hard exercise," I did what was natural—I consulted a physician—in this case, a practicing cardiologist, Dr. Jonathan Alexander, Director of the Cardiovascular Rehabilitation Program at Danbury Hospital in Connecticut. Dr. Alexander is also an associate clinical professor of medicine at the Yale University School of Medicine, a fellow of the American College of Cardiology and a member of the American College of Sports Medicine.

*Fast:* What is the most beneficial part of exercise?

*Dr. Alexander:* I would say it's the *training effect,* the effect of regular, sustained and strenuous exercise on the body.

*Fast:* Just what is the *training effect?*

*Dr. Alexander:* Let me put it this way; if you think of the body as a car, you could liken the *training effect* to a thorough tune-up. Afterwards the car works better and more economically. It conserves energy by getting more mileage for the gas used. Once you've achieved the *training effect,* your heart will work more efficiently. It will beat at a slower rate during exercise and at rest.

*Fast:* Now if I wanted to reach this *training effect,* what would I have to do?

*Dr. Alexander:* You'd have to pick a form of exercise that increased your heart rate, raised it to a certain level and kept it there for thirty to forty minutes.

*Fast:* What is that level?

*Dr. Alexander:* That depends on your age. It's seventy percent of what is called the age-predicted maximum.

*Fast:* Could you explain what you mean by the age-predicted maximum?

*Dr. Alexander:* It's simply the maximum rate at which your heart will beat. This changes with age. When you're twenty-five years old, for example, your heart can reach two hundred beats a minute if you exercise strenuously. If you're fifty years old, however, it will only reach a hundred seventy one beats. Here's a chart that shows the maximum beat reached at various ages. The last column shows seventy percent of that beat.

| Age | Maximum heart beat during very strenuous exercise | Seventy percent of the maximum beat. The pulse rate you should strive for to get the training effect |
|-----|-----|-----|
| 25 | 200 | 140 |
| 26 | 198 | 138 |
| 27 | 197 | 138 |
| 28 | 196 | 137 |
| 29 | 195 | 136 |
| 30 | 194 | 136 |

| | | |
|---|---|---|
| 31 | 192 | 134 |
| 32 | 191 | 134 |
| 33 | 190 | 133 |
| 34 | 189 | 132 |
| 35 | 188 | 132 |
| 36 | 186 | 130 |
| 37 | 185 | 130 |
| 38 | 184 | 129 |
| 39 | 183 | 128 |
| 40 | 182 | 127 |
| 41 | 180 | 126 |
| 42 | 179 | 125 |
| 43 | 178 | 125 |
| 44 | 177 | 124 |
| 45 | 176 | 123 |
| 46 | 175 | 123 |
| 47 | 174 | 122 |
| 48 | 173 | 121 |
| 49 | 172 | 120 |
| 50 | 171 | 120 |
| 51 | 169 | 118 |
| 52 | 168 | 118 |
| 53 | 167 | 117 |
| 54 | 166 | 116 |
| 55 | 165 | 116 |
| 56 | 163 | 114 |
| 57 | 162 | 113 |
| 58 | 161 | 113 |
| 59 | 160 | 112 |
| 60 | 159 | 111 |
| 61 | 157 | 110 |
| 62 | 156 | 109 |
| 63 | 155 | 109 |
| 64 | 154 | 108 |

| 65 | 153 | 107 |
| 66 | 152 | 106 |
| 67 | 151 | 106 |
| 68 | 150 | 105 |
| 69 | 149 | 104 |
| 70 | 148 | 104 |

*Fast:* How does the *training effect* work in relation to the chart?

*Dr. Alexander:* Say, for example, that you're thirty years old. Your age-predicted heart rate is a hundred ninety-four beats a minute. Seventy percent of that is a hundred thirty-six. To get a *training effect,* you must exercise until your heart beats a hundred thirty-six times per minute and keep that up for thirty to forty-five minutes. Do this three times a week and you have achieved the *training effect.*

*Fast:* Now can anyone go out and do this on his own without having a doctor recommend it?

*Dr. Alexander:* If he's in reasonable health with no heart problem, I see no reason why he can't do it on his own.

*Fast:* What about someone who has led a sedentary life up to that point?

*Dr. Alexander:* It's a good idea for anyone over the age of thirty-five starting strenuous exercise for the first time to get a stress test, if only to exclude the possibility of coronary disease without symptoms. The same is true of someone with a family history of cardiovascular disease. A lot of people say, "Hey, I'm going to start getting myself in shape," and they plunge into an exercise program without having their hearts checked out. Then one day, wham! Some of them drop dead out on the track or in the field or the gym.

*Fast:* Let's get back to the *training effect*. What exercise is best for someone who wants to achieve it?

*Dr. Alexander:* It has to be an exercise that will make you exert yourself enough to raise your heartbeat. Swimming is the best exercise, because it not only does that, but also puts no stress on the body joints. It does the least damage to our muscles and bones, and there's no danger of being bitten by a dog or run over by a car.

*Fast:* But it does require a pool.

*Dr. Alexander:* True. Well, after swimming, I'd say running or jogging is best. For someone sixty-five or older, jogging combined with walking is excellent. At that age, you should start out with strenuous walking and build up to a jog.

*Fast:* For a younger person, what about biking?

*Dr. Alexander:* Biking is excellent. Strenuous dancing is excellent too. You know, cross-country skiing is one of the best exercises, far better than downhill skiing. Racquetball and handball are both good. Tennis isn't so good unless you play very hard and fast, but the average tennis game won't give you the *training effect*. However, squash, paddle ball and handball are all good. In the competitive sports, soccer and basketball are excellent. Football is not so good, not enough sustained activity. Touch football is better, especially if you do a lot of running. Track and field sports are fine, but golf, that old standby of the older set, is useless . . . particularly useless if you use a golf cart.

*Fast:* What about weightlifting?

*Dr. Alexander:* It does nothing to achieve the *training effect*. Its only value is cosmetic. Remember, you're not sustaining your heart rate when you lift a weight suddenly. What happens is that your blood pressure shoots up. Because of this, weight-lifting can be potentially dangerous, especially to someone with cardiovascular disease. There is, incidentally, a syndrome in which young people with hypertrophied, enlarged hearts can die suddenly if they lift any excess weight. This should point out the importance of getting a physical examination before you exercise, even when you're young.

*Fast:* Would you go so far as to recommend a physical examination for anyone who goes into sports or exercise, regardless of age?

*Dr. Alexander:* I think it would be a very good idea for anyone who suddenly becomes active and tries for the *training effect.*

*Fast:* I've noticed, in interviewing women who've gone into weightlifting, that they don't seem to develop the extraordinary muscles men do.

*Dr. Alexander:* There is a limit to the muscle size in women under normal hormonal conditions. Of course, if you give women androgens, as the Eastern European countries occasionally do, you can increase their muscle size and strength.

*Fast:* You confirm something I said in an earlier chapter, that if women exercise they won't get bulging muscles.

*Dr. Alexander:* That's right. Oh, I've seen women athletes and ballet dancers with well-developed thigh muscles, but there is a limit, and they don't become as grotesque as male weightlifters. You know, when a weightlifter stops working out, the muscles he has built up begin to atrophy and are replaced by fat cells. Unless he goes on lifting weights all his life, he'll get those fatty breasts that hang down and a belly that bulges over.

*Fast:* Is there one form of exercise you recommend

to your patients, one you favor above others?

*Dr. Alexander:* A lot of patients ask me what kind of exercise they should do, and I make all kinds of recommendations, but in the final analysis, it must be individualized. The exercise must fit the person, and the important thing is to enjoy whatever exercise you are doing.

*Fast:* What do you do with someone who just doesn't enjoy any exercise?

*Dr. Alexander:* Well, there always seems to be something they can do. As an example, everyone rides a bike at some point in his life, and it's something he can always get back to. He may not enjoy the sweating aspects of it, but it's a skill he knows, and it can be done with other family members. For the exercise-hater, I try to encourage a family-type of sport, one the whole family can get into. I suggest they join the Y or a swim club.

Another thing, everyone walks to some degree. You can work that into an exercise routine. I encourage some people to start climbing stairs instead of using the elevator, to walk instead of using cabs.

*Fast:* When you talk about climbing stairs, how many flights do you mean? One or two, or ten or more? And doesn't climbing stairs put a sudden strain on the heart?

*Dr. Alexander:* Yes, if you don't build it up gradually, it puts a strain on you, but carefully increased, stair climbing is a very strenuous form of exercise and great for conditioning the heart. The only problem is the difficulty of sustaining it for forty minutes. You'd probably have to climb a skyscraper for that!

*Fast:* Let's consider the absolutely sedentary guy again. You start him out walking, right?

*Dr. Alexander:* Right. Start him out walking to work, or walking around the block; a brisk walk that will get the heart rate up to a respectable level.

*Fast:* With any of these exercises, like this sedentary walker, isn't there the problem that the exercise may be seasonal? Is he still going to stick to it when the rain comes or the temperature zooms down?

*Dr. Alexander:* This is a problem, and a lot of people ask, what can I do in the winter when it's too cold outside? That's the time to think about home equipment, rowing machines, stationary bicycles. It could take the boredom out of exercise. You could watch TV while you're on the machine, or listen to music.

*Fast:* Now I know you say weightlifting is bad, but what about working out with five-pound weights to limber up?

*Dr. Alexander:* They're excellent. They can maintain a certain level of muscle tone, but you know, I still think the most important thing is finding a form of exercise that you can enjoy doing, and one you can do year round.

*Fast:* That brings up something else. Is there extra pressure on the body during the winter? Does the cold make it more difficult to exercise?

*Dr. Alexander:* Yes. The body has to work harder. It is stressed to a greater degree. To protect the body against the cold, the circulation is conserved. Less blood goes out to the skin and limbs. Because of that there is an increase in blood pressure and the heart rate goes up.

*Fast:* Then if you jog, say two miles a day in warm weather, should you cut the distance down in cold weather?

*Dr. Alexander:* You probably should, and you

should also be aware that there are risks to jogging in extreme cold. There are injuries that the cold can bring on. You can suck in very cold air and damage your lungs, or you can get frostbite of the nose.

*Fast:* That doesn't surprise me. But the big advantage in jogging year round, it seems, is that it's available to everyone.

*Dr. Alexander:* It would be nice if all exercise were free and available to everyone. Jogging is, and so is biking, aside from buying the bike. Swimming is free only if you happen to live near water, but even if you have to pay to join a pool or health club, you should look on the exercise and the money spent for it as an important investment in your health.

*Fast:* Then you really think it's worthwhile buying a stationary bicycle or a rowing machine or any indoor exerciser?

*Dr. Alexander:* It is. It's also worthwhile to join a gym or a racquetball club. Exercise should be a regular part of your life. I know there will always be some people who consider it a burden, but an exercise program is a form of discipline. There's a saying among runners, "No pain, no gain!" In a sense that applies to all exercise. If you don't work hard at it, you won't get any benefit out of it.

*Fast:* You mentioned the psychological benefits of exercise. What are they?

*Dr. Alexander:* A number of studies have pointed out a strong association between physical fitness and emotional health. Exercise, competitive or not, is a very effective way of releasing tension and stress. It's a good way to deal with the pressures of a job. Also, people sleep better on days when they exercise. This makes sense when you consider that loss of sleep is associated with stress. Relieve the stress, help the sleep. People who exercise regularly also derive more benefit from their sleep. They dream dreams that allow them to work out their frustrations and tensions.

*Fast:* You spoke of the discipline of exercise. Is that a factor?

*Dr. Alexander:* Anything that requires a certain amount of discipline, anything you *must* do three times a week, has benefits in your work life and in your home life. It's a sort of 'ordering.' Hostility, anger, tension, rejection, anxiety, middle-age life crises—all these are eased or even eliminated by exercise. This is well-substantiated by psychological reports. Since stress and tension are coronary risk factors (causes of heart disease), their relief takes us back in a circle to the relief of heart disease.

*Fast:* Can you really say, then, that exercise allows us to live longer, that it prevents heart disease?

*Dr. Alexander:* That's an extremely controversial question. I feel that it does, but I don't have any hard scientific proof. We know that with regular exercise the HDL goes up and the serum cholesterol comes down.

*Fast:* What is the HDL?

*Dr. Alexander:* HDL stands for High Density Lipoproteins, one of the components of cholesterol. A lipoprotein is a fat attached to a protein.

*Fast:* Is there any relationship between HDL and heart disease?

*Dr. Alexander:* First let me talk about serum cholesterol and heart disease. Many years ago it was discovered that people with a high serum cholesterol had a higher incidence of coronary artery disease. Several studies showed that this was a clear-cut relationship. Therefore a high serum cholesterol is considered one of the major risk factors for heart disease. Two other risk factors are high blood pressure and smoking. However, researchers have wondered whether high cholesterol in the blood is the *cause,* or simply a marker for something else.

*Fast:* If that is so, then getting the serum cholesterol down wouldn't necessarily affect the plaques of cholesterol that narrow the blood-vessel walls.

*Dr. Alexander:* That's right. The serum cholesterol may simply be saying the patient has a certain type of metabolism, and that metabolism could be the guilty factor. I believe that in some ways a high serum cholesterol does indeed reflect what is happening at the level of the artery, but I don't believe it's the complete picture. I think there's something else going on. You see, people with normal cholesterol levels can still have severe coronary disease, and people with high cholesterol levels may be free of coronary artery disease.

*Fast:* Now what about HDL? How does that fit into the picture?

*Dr. Alexander:* HDL is a better marker for coronary artery disease than cholesterol. The higher your HDL, the *less* chance you have of a heart attack.

*Fast:* Is there a value beyond which nobody gets a heart attack?

*Dr. Alexander:* Some researchers feel that sixty or seventy is the lower limit. Others consider the ratio of HDL to cholesterol important. Most important, I think, is the fact that several studies have shown that regular exercise will lower the cholesterol level and raise the HDL. My personal feeling is that regular exercise does prevent the progression of coronary artery disease.

*Fast:* Have you, in your practice, found that people

who do have heart attacks are more sedentary?

*Dr. Alexander:* Yes. There is no doubt about it. I think that a sedentary life spells eventual trouble for the heart. Usually the heart patient I see is overweight, has poorly controlled high blood pressure, is under a lot of stress and is sedentary.

*Fast:* But couldn't the fact that he's sedentary have come about because he's overweight and under stress?

*Dr. Alexander:* It's hard to know which causes which.

*Fast:* It seems to me that another point that confuses the issue is that if you give the overweight, sedentary patient a program of exercise, you're going to lower his stress and he'll probably begin losing weight.

*Dr. Alexander:* It's very difficult to isolate all these factors.

*Fast:* But even if exercise didn't help, it certainly couldn't hurt!

*Dr. Alexander:* I think most cardiologists are beginning to believe that some form of exercise, whether it be on the training level or not, is important to a healthy lifestyle.

*Fast:* Outside of heart disease, are there any other physical conditions that are benefited by exercise?

*Dr. Alexander:* Diabetes is. Recent studies have shown that diabetics who exercise on a regular basis require less insulin.

*Fast:* Couldn't this be because of the loss of weight?

*Dr. Alexander;* Presumably it's not only weight loss, but also better utilization of their enzymatic system. It has to do with better functioning of the insulin within the body.

*Fast:* Is there any hint that exercise can *prevent*

diabetes?

*Dr. Alexander:* No, but I suspect it could retard the onset of the disease. Some doctors have advocated exercise for people with a variety of lung disorders with the understanding that there's a minimum amount of benefit that can be gained.

*Fast:* What about asthma?

*Dr. Alexander:* I would not advise asthmatics to go out and exercise. There is a syndrome called exercise-induced asthma. Some people are actually allergic to exercise, and one of the manifestations of this allergy is asthma. Heart problems, diabetes, some lung conditions—those are the major physiological conditions that benefit from exercise, but I would extend the benefits to all emotional disorders. We physicians should ask ourselves, "What is the role of the emotions in the production of other illnesses?" Cancer, for instance. A lot of current research seems to indicate a connection between cancer and emotional stress. If there is such a connection, and exercise helps the psyche, won't it also help the cancer?

*Fast:* Has exercise any beneficial effect on sex?

*Dr. Alexander:* Yes. Exercise can cause an improvement in sexual performance, not a quantitative improvement, but a qualitative one.

*Fast:* How does that work?

*Dr. Alexander:* Sex is sometimes a way of relieving tension. When that happens, it becomes quick and joyless. There's a driving need to have sex and an orgasm quickly. It becomes only a release to tension. But if one relieves the tension in other ways through exercise, then sex isn't necessary as a tension release, and it can become a different experience, richer and more meaningful. It also tones up the body and from that standpoint it helps. A healthy body is better able to function sexually. But a word of caution. Sex should not be considered in the list of exercises that achieve the *training effect*. It's very hard to indulge in enough sex to maintain a heart rate a hundred and forty beats for thirty minutes!

*Fast:* Not unless you expand sexual exercise to hunting down the "other" and wining and dining him or her. But for the record, what are the number of calories you expend on sex?

*Dr. Alexander:* That depends on whether it's extra-marital or conjugal.

*Fast:* More extramaritally, I suppose?

*Dr. Alexander:* Obviously, because there is more excitement, more strain; but in any sexual encounter you don't expend a great number of calories—two hundred at the most. I think it's best to save sex for pleasure and exercise for health, knowing that exercise will improve the pleasure of sex.

# 15

# THE ULTIMATE EQUATION

### The No-Diet Diet, The Human Machine

"Every day in every way I am growing fatter and flabbier," Rona, an attractive but plump young woman, told me. "I can't diet and I can't exercise. I'm a wipeout, a deadbeat, a failure!"

I said, "Slow down. What's the trouble? Why don't you diet? Have you tried?"

"Have I tried?" She sighed and shook her head. "I have tried, believe me. I get a diet and start it, and then I get so tense about whether or not it will work that I begin to eat everything in sight to relieve my tension. The same is true of exercise. I worry about whether I'm getting the *training effect* you told me about, whether I'll have time to exercise, whether it's going to rain and keep me from jogging—I tell you, I worry so much I never get to the exercise."

"Let's take one problem at a time," I suggested. "You say dieting gets you tense? Why don't you take off the weight without dieting?"

Rona looked at me, startled. "Have you flipped out? How am I supposed to do that?"

I had given Rona my FATAWAY diet along with a thorough explanation of how calories work. That had been almost a month ago. "Why don't you simply forget about the diet," I told her, "and concentrate on the calories. Count calories. Count how many you take in each day during normal eating. Then begin to trim some off. See what you can do without a cookie here or an ice-cream cone there. Take one slice of bread less, omit a pat of butter. You know that business about not seeing the forest for the trees? Turn the cliché around. Deliberately try to ignore the forest. Concentrate on the trees. In other words, forget the total picture. Forget the concept of a diet. Just nibble away at the calories.''

Rona was doubtful, but she had failed at so many diets that she was desperate enough to try anything. "Remember," I told her, "you aren't trying to diet. If you don't want to cut out a baked potato or an extra slice of beef, then don't. Just be aware of the caloric count of what you do eat, and above all, remember that this is not a diet. You're not out to lose weight, just to trim off some calories. What's more, don't weigh yourself.''

"How will I know if I'm gaining or losing if I don't weigh in?" Rona asked plaintively.

"That's not important. The whole point is not to know. So I absolutely forbid you to step on a scale!''

It took a bit more arguing, but finally Rona agreed to do just what I had suggested. After the first week she reported with some surprise that it was easy. "I don't get tense about it, because I've taken you at your word and decided I'm not out to lose weight, just cut calories. I don't know how much I've cut out, but like you said, I'm nibbling away at them, and it's better than nibbling at my usual munchies. I carry a pocket calorie counter with me. Like I've discovered that a jelly doughnut has two-hundred calories. Imagine that! I used to have one with my coffee at every coffee break, but they don't taste as good, now that I know what they represent in cold calories . . . or should that be hot calories?"

The next week Rona reported, "I'm losing it. By God, I can't believe it, but it's coming off!"

"Hey, I thought we decided no scales?"

"Heaven forbid I should step on a scale!" She threw up her hands. "Oh no, it's just the way my pants fit. If I keep this up, I should really get in shape."

"Why not? There's nothing to worry about as long as you don't diet."

What I had done with Rona was remove the Damoclean sword of a failed diet that had always hung over her. Once she understood the simple principle of caloric equivalents, she began to change her eating patterns by counting her calories and cutting them. A formal diet is simply a disciplined way of cutting calories, and of course many people, unlike Rona, need the discipline of a rigid diet.

I knew a writer once who could only turn out a script if he had a tight deadline. The deadline supplied the same type of discipline that a rigid diet does for the average person who wants to lose weight. But there are many of us, like Rona, who cannot function within the framework of a diet—or a deadline. I also know many writers who feel trapped and crippled by deadlines. They have to produce slowly at their own pace.

For people like that, a thorough understanding of the caloric equivalence of food will allow them to make their own diet with little effort.

Although, for a week or two, almost any diet can be indulged in without harm, the best type of diet, in the long run, is a well-balanced one, well-balanced in nutritional terms. Cutting out calories here and there will usually result in a diet much like the one you usually eat, but caloric intake is pared down to help you lose weight.

The lesson we learn very quickly when we begin to diet is that there's no gain without pain, as Dr. Alexander said about exercise. The pain may be on a physical level, for example hunger cramps, or it may come on a deeper, psychological level. This is particularly true when eating serves other functions besides appeasing hunger. Food may represent love and affection, or affluence, a sign that you've made it, or it may even be a status symbol. Giving up some food, when food is linked to any of these things, is very difficult. But a true understanding of how much potential body fat there is in each type of food makes giving it up easier. Learning the basic principle behind every successful diet—cut down your caloric intake and you burn up your stored fat—allows you to apply that principle, as Rona did, without the sense that she was actually dieting.

There must be a caveat here. There are some few people who do have glandular problems, and for them the simple calorie-fat equation doesn't hold. They will eventually lose weight if they cut enough calories, but for them it is a much harder process. Of course there are also an unfortunate few who cannot gain weight for different glandular reasons. Their bodies burn everything up far too efficiently. Fortunately, there are very, very few people in either of these situations, and the odds are that you are not one of them.

Rona was told to forget about dieting and concentrate on cutting calories. Another good piece of advice on dieting was given to me by a cagey psychiatrist. "Never tell anyone when you go on a diet. Deny that you are dieting, and if you're complimented on how you look say, oh, it must be this new suit or dress. This is to do away with all the sabotage that will come your way once well-meaning but foolish friends learn that you're on a diet."

However, in all fairness, another equally cagey psychiatrist advised me, "Let everyone know. Box yourself in so that you have no way out. Boast of your diet and what it will accomplish. In this way, you'll shame yourself into staying on it. If you break it, you'll end up looking very foolish."

This advice would go for the person who favors a rigid diet. It would never do for someone like Rona. The tension of broadcasting her goals and the focus of everyone's attention would do her in in no time.

In turn, the caloric principle of diet should be taken one step farther into the realm of exercise. Learning the caloric equivalent of a walk around the block, a ten-mile bike trip, a run through the park, or a workout on the handball court will allow you to take off even more weight in the unstructured manner. It becomes a matter of burning up more calories.

These two principles, the caloric equivalent of food and of exercise, are all we need to keep our weight under control. If we want to add to this the tuning up of our bodies, we need a bit more knowledge. We have to know the amount of exercise that will produce the *training effect*. It's an interesting bit of trivia that the exercise equivalent of one dish of ice cream, twenty minutes of running, will give most of us the *training effect* if we do it three times a week!

It is also interesting to realize that if you can forget the formal diet along with those pressures it brings; if you can ease up on your impatience that the weight isn't coming off fast enough and stop agonizing over the fact that so-and-so lost so-many pounds to your so-few; if you can relax and be satisfied with your caloric counting and approach losing weight in an unhurried way, you may very well be taking an important step towards improving your life.

If you can do this successfully, you may be changing your behavior from what heart specialists call "Type A behavior," the behavior of the competitive, driven, aggressive and impatient personality, to "Type B," the behavior of the relaxed, laid-back personality. The incidence of coronary heart disease is twice as great with "Type A" as it is with "Type B." It's something to think about.

## The Human Machine

I am not trying to say, by any means, that it's wrong to go on a rigid diet such as the FATAWAY diet. Dieting like this can obviously be of tremendous value, not only in taking off excess weight, but also in learning to rethink your entire approach to food. I stress the caloric principle because it teaches the dieter the basics of eating. The FATAWAY diet is not a fad diet that may fill you dangerously full of protein while it deprives you of fat or carbohydrates. We humans are omnivorous, which means we do well on a mix of animal and vegetable foods. We can survive on a diet that is mostly meat, but we pay a price. To get along on an all-vegetable diet we must maintain a sophisticated mix of proteins. The best type of diet for reducing or for living is one like the FATAWAY, which includes some animal protein, fish, fowl or meat, carbohydrates that are not refined, and fats.

To take off weight, we should simply cut down on *all* of these, not on one. We should continue to feed our bodies the correct balance, just less food. The best technique for dieting should teach us how to eat properly once we stop dieting, how to maintain not only our proper weight, but also our proper health.

As for exercise, it is no longer an isolated action we can separate from how we eat. It is firmly linked to diet, not only because we must eat to move, but also because the amount of exercise we do is directly proportional to the number of calories we burn. The rough equation is: Calories taken in minus calories-burned equals calories-stored. If the result of the equation is negative, it means calories are lost. The calories taken in are our diets. The calories burned are a combination of exercise and body function. The calories stored is the weight we put on, and the calories lost is the weight we take off. The equation should balance during the normal course of life. Out of balance, we take weight off or put it on. Whether we balance it or leave it unbalanced is our choice.

There is another positive aspect to exercise. It can improve the content of our blood, the cholesterol balance, and through this the well-being of our circulatory system. And it can also tune up our bodies.

This is a body book and contains a great deal of thought and experience about the body, some derived from medical research, some from authorities in the fields of diet, exercise and medicine, and some from people who have lived and solved the problems all of us face.

We owe a debt of gratitude to our bodies because they are the wonderful machines that allow us to experience life. That gratitude should impel us to take care of those machines, to keep them tuned to precision, to make sure the load they carry through life is not excessive.

But the need to take care of the human machine goes beyond gratitude. It extends to the entire experience of life. How you react to life, how you live it, your emotional well-being, and to a great extent your happiness, all depend on that machine. Any journey in a rusty, creaky, inefficient vehicle is a dreadful experience. The same journey in a well-oiled, well-tuned, efficient machine is a joy. After all, we only go round once. Let's do it in style.